PURRFECT CATCH

THE MYSTERIES OF MAX 40

NIC SAINT

PURRFECT CATCH

The Mysteries of Max 40

Copyright © 2021 by Nic Saint

Edited by Chereese Graves

www.nicsaint.com

Give feedback on the book at: info@nicsaint.com

facebook.com/nicsaintauthor
@nicsaintauthor

First Edition

Printed in the U.S.A

A deep sense of satisfaction spread through George Calhoun. It was the same satisfaction he remembered from his bachelor days—those wild days of yore when the gutter press had often referred to him as the world's most eligible bachelor. But ever since he got hitched, not only was he no longer a bachelor, it was almost as if the world had forgotten about him.

The tabloids had stopped writing about him, the paparazzi had stopped chasing him, and, most importantly, the girls had stopped lavishing him with their attentions and had redirected their interest elsewhere. Young whippersnappers like Timothée Chalamet or Tom Holland were now the talk of the town, and of George Calhoun they only spoke with mild mockery, as if he was the ultimate has-been. Nothing but a punchline at parties.

Once upon a time he'd been the leader of the rat pack, a group of young up-and-coming men who were infamous for their wild parties, with no woman safe from their flirtatious ways or roving eye. Often were the times when he woke up in a strange bed, next to an unfamiliar but gorgeous babe, and couldn't remember how he got there.

And now, thanks to a twist of fate, once more he was reliving his glory days. He smiled at the voluptuous blonde who lay next to him by the pool. They'd just made love like animals in heat, and he felt exhausted but sated. This old dog still had it. He hadn't forgotten how to satisfy a woman and make her cry out in satisfaction.

"Hey, you," he now said lazily as he enjoyed the sun beating down on his naked self.

"Hey, yourself," she purred, and as he admired her features, she rearranged them for his full benefit.

"Was it as great for you as it was for me?" he asked, putting that seductive tone in his voice for which he'd been so famous once upon a not so long ago.

"Oh, Georgie, it was magical!" she said and moved closer to him.

They shared a kiss that started out chaste but gradually became a little less so. And soon he was ready for round two, or was it round three? Frankly he'd lost count.

His wife was out with the twins, and he'd given the staff the afternoon off, so he and Tammy had the place to themselves. The pool was cool and inviting, but Tammy even more so, and then once again he threw caution to the wind and gave himself up to her sultry wiles and ear-splitting moans.

No one had ever expected him to settle down and get married, much less produce offspring, but that was exactly what had happened. When he met the smart and very attractive Anna, who was a successful barrister in London, it had taken him a lot of work to persuade her he wasn't just another hot-shot Hollywood star, but that he was actually serious about her. And he was. Still to this day he worshipped the ground she walked on. But she was now the mother of his kids, and they'd settled down in the sort of routine he'd abhorred all his life, and so when the opportunity presented itself to engage in some friskiness with a hot neighbor, he'd found it hard to resist. He now considered it a present to himself for being such a devoted husband and father. And of course he almost felt as if he needed to prove to himself that he still had it. And obviously he did. In spades! At least if Tammy's loud whimperings were any reference. Good thing his closest neighbor was two hundred yards away, safely obscured from view behind a tall perimeter fence.

And as he gave himself up to reliving the sins of his ill-spent younger years, suddenly he became aware of a familiar sound. It was a sound he'd become accustomed to from living in LA, but out here in the Hamptons it was the first time he'd ever encountered it.

And as he glanced up at the clear blue sky, shielding his eyes from the blazing sun, that's when he saw it: a drone, hovering directly over him and Tammy!

He inwardly cursed, and immediately realized the pickle he was in. For it was exactly this kind of drone the paparazzi liked to employ to snap compromising shots of unsuspecting celebrities and sell them to the highest bidder.

Tammy, who'd become aware of his diminishing involvement, now also glanced up, and when she spotted that same drone, cursed even louder than he did.

"Look away," he advised immediately. "As long as they don't get your face on camera..."

"Too late, Georgie," she said ruefully. "Looks like they've got some great footage."

And as he got up with some effort—he'd recently suffered a back hernia—one of the many things that reminded him he wasn't the man he used to be—he picked up a rock and threw it at the drone, hoping to knock the darn thing straight out of the sky.

Immediately the drone banked, and then flew off, but presumably not before snapping another few choice images of the famous George Calhoun, his manhood on display, engaging in relations with a woman who was very obviously not his wife.

"Dammit," he said as he watched the pesky drone fly off. Then he repeated the same phrase, but only with more heat and more vigor, shaking a fist at that searing blue sky.

$\clubsuit$

Some men, when they search out the company of their friends, like to go fishing. Other men watch football on as big a screen as they can afford, enjoying beer and wieners in the process. Still other men buy themselves expensive toys to show off. And it was in this latter category that Tex Poole firmly belonged. The small-town doctor had recently become the proud owner of a drone, and now felt the need to show it off to his son-in-law and his brother-in-law. After all, why else would you buy an expensive useless gadget?

And so it was that Tex, equipped with his spanking new drone, complete with FAA license, his local permit fees paid in full, found himself in their local park with Chase and Alec, to demonstrate the benefits of his drone. It was one of those state-of-the-art drones, with top-of-the-line camera, that you can use to photograph the area from an angle which hitherto was only reserved for birds or the owners of small planes. He had installed an app on his tablet, and as he launched the drone up in the air, the three men stood staring in awe how the drone captured the world below with crystal-clear, HD-quality imagery.

"Amazing," Chase commented as the drone flew over the park, and sent some very nice footage of the tops of the trees back to the three men huddled around Tex's tablet.

"Such a clear picture," said Alec. He'd suggested they take advantage of the drone's maiden voyage to spend an afternoon at the beach... Until he discovered that their local beaches were off-limits for Unmanned Aerial Vehicles, as drones are officially called, between Memorial Day and Labor Day. And as Chief of Police, it behooved Alec to follow the rules. Still, when the drone now moved a little lower, and two scantily-dressed ladies came into view who were enjoying a little sunshine, Alec appeared a little overexcited.

"We're not going to use this revolutionary new technology to ogle the ladies, Alec," said Tex censoriously, and instead steered his drone inland, away from the park.

"Yes, Alec," Chase chimed in. "What is Charlene going to say?"

"I was just checking to see if they were applying sunscreen," Alec sputtered.

"Sure you were," said Tex as he intently watched the screen, to gauge where his drone was now flying. It looked as if the nifty little gadget was hovering over a large villa or mansion, and as soon as a pool came into view, he knew he was probably looking into the backyard of one of the movers and shakers the Hamptons are so rightly famous for.

"Will you look at this place," said Alec with a whistle. He was of course intimately familiar with the goings-on in their cozy little community, but even he was often surprised by the kind of wealth that was on display in their corner of the world.

"I'll bet that's Steven Spielberg's place," said Chase as he tapped the tablet.

"Please don't touch the screen," Tex lamented as the image immediately zoomed in on the spot Chase had tapped.

"Sorry, Dad," said Chase with a grin. The cop was not a native of Hampton Cove, but had lived there long enough to realize that looking into the backyard of a member of the local economic or cultural elite was not a good idea, considering privacy laws and such, so he added, "Better move along. We don't want to get this guy's lawyers on our ass."

"Uh-huh," said Tex as he fiddled with the controls. He was still a little uncertain as to what the exact procedure was to make the drone adhere to his command, and as he pressed this on-screen button then that, the pool, on which Chase had inadvertently zoomed in, proved to be the scene of some strenuous activity of a very frivolous nature.

"Are they..." said Alec as he frowned at the image on the tablet, which now focused on the couple lying next to the pool.

"Looks like they are," said Chase, his infectious grin widening.

"Um, how do I make it move away from there?" said Tex, as the drone wouldn't budge, no matter which button he touched.

But both Chase and Alec were too busy staring at the scene to offer him any advice. For the imagery displayed on the tablet was straight out of some X-rated movie, with both man and woman completely devoid of garments, and locked in a very tight embrace.

"Oh, dear..." said Tex as he, too, was now consumed with the footage as it played out before his eyes. Now Tex, being a doctor, was intimately familiar with the human anatomy, but even he had to admit that these were two prime specimens of the human race. The man was gray-haired but had clearly done his utmost to stay in fine physical shape, and the woman was one of those pneumatic blondes with assets that sent the blood pressure of the three men skyrocketing into the danger zone. And like three naughty boys, they sat there staring at the Kama Sutra demonstration with red ears and even redder cheeks.

Until finally Tex cleared his throat and said, "I think we better move along, guys."

"Yeah, I guess you're right," said Alec slowly.

And then, all of a sudden, the gray-haired man must have become aware that he was being watched, for he glanced up, straight into the camera of the overflying drone.

"Well, I'll be damned," said Chase. "That's George Calhoun!"

"And that lady definitely is not Anna Calhoun," Alec grunted.

"Okay, so how do I make it fly away?" asked Tex as once again he was helplessly fiddling with the controls. He should have stayed safely in the park, he now realized, like all the regulations advised. Instead, he'd probably broken about a dozen privacy laws.

The man in the picture, who was indeed the famous silver fox George Calhoun, hero of so many great movies, and also happily married father of twins, now picked up a rock and threw it at Tex's drone, a clear sign he wasn't all that happy with this sudden intrusion.

"Have you tried this button?" asked Chase, as he pressed one of the jiggly little controls on the screen. Immediately the drone responded and flew on, leaving the irate actor and his girlfriend behind, with George staring up at the drone in helpless rage.

The three men now shared a look of significance and even as Tex heaved a sigh of relief, Alec said, "I think we better don't mention this to anyone, fellas."

"My lips are sealed," Tex wholeheartedly agreed.

"If anyone found out that George Calhoun is cheating on Anna…" said Chase, as he shook his head.

"So it's agreed?" asked Tex. "This never happened?"

And then the three men shook hands. George Calhoun might be a cheat and a lousy husband, but as far as Tex was concerned, his secret was safe.

The incident had passed, and his drone was still intact, and so was his legal position.

Luckily there was no way George could ever find out who this particular drone belonged to, since he probably hadn't been able to see the registration number printed on the side. And so as he managed to steer his nifty gadget back to the park, to take in more innocent landscapes, this time devoid of cheating Hollywood stars, Tex knew that his purchase would give him many hours of enjoyment in the weeks and months to come.

*E*ven though generally speaking my life hasn't exactly been a bed of thorns, there are still things I experience from time to time that every cat the world over dreads. And one of those things is a visit to the vet. As a rule, Odelia, my human, knows and respects my absolute abhorrence of vets and only schedules a visit when she has no other recourse. But at least once a year she takes us for a visit anyway, just to see if everything is in order.

"It's just like with a car, see?" Gran explained this concept to me. "You need to get your car inspected once a year, even though it's still running just fine, and isn't leaking any oil and the engine isn't making any strange noises. The same goes for cats, or even humans. I go to the doctor once a year, or the dentist, and so should you. Just in case there's something wrong, so you can get ahead of the disease. It's called preventive healthcare."

It all sounded very suspicious to me. For one thing, cats aren't cars. We don't lose oil, and our engines don't sputter or make strange noises, unless you like to call our purring a strange noise, and in a sense it is, but not indicative of disease but of satisfaction. And secondly, since cats aren't humans either, why would we go to a doctor when we're not sick? It doesn't make sense. But then a lot of things humans do fall into that category.

"But I don't want to go to the vet, Max," said Dooley, who shares my dim view of vets.

"It'll be fine," said Brutus, our butch black friend. "We're the picture of health, so Vena is bound to take one look at us and tell Odelia to come back next year."

"I don't know, beautiful," said Harriet, Brutus's white Persian girlfriend. "Have you seen Max lately?"

They all looked at me now, and I frowned. "What do you mean by that?" I asked.

"Harriet is right," said Brutus. "You have gained a lot of weight lately, Maxie baby."

"No, I haven't. If anything, I've lost weight. Lots of weight." If there's something I'm particularly sensitive about, it's my weight. And that's because I'm one of those cats with big bones, you see, and as a consequence I may look and feel just that little bit heavier than other cats, but it's not something that can be remedied by dieting, which often seems to be the only solution Vena, our town's go-to veterinarian, likes to suggest.

"Do you still fit through the pet flap?" asked Harriet, a look of concern on her face.

I rolled my eyes. "Of course I fit through the pet flap, Harriet. Here, let me demonstrate how well I fit through the pet flap."

The pet flap seems to have become some kind of gauge or measure of how big I am. And I have to admit, there was a time when I didn't fit through the thing, but that's because Tex, who built it, is a lousy handyman, and made it much too tight.

I proceeded to confidently stride up to the pet flap. But as

I approached, I started to experience a niggling doubt. I don't know if you've had this, but one moment you're fine, while the next, and especially when people start to question your capacity to produce a certain result, suddenly doubt starts to creep in, and that thing that you could do with your eyes closed, so to speak, suddenly becomes a hurdle that seems unpassable.

And so as I walked up to that pet flap, suddenly I wondered whether I did fit through the thing. But then I remembered distinctly how I'd fit through it just the day before. And I smiled and was at peace again. Until I approached a little closer still, and suddenly doubt reared its ugly head once more. Was it the day before... or the week before? Or even last month? I now seemed to remember I'd been using the kitchen door a lot lately, or even the sliding glass door in the living room, as Odelia often leaves it open for us.

But as I tentatively put my head through the flap, I relaxed again and knew I had nothing to worry about. I'd once heard Odelia tell Chase, when she made him privy to some of the secrets from the mysterious world of felines, that if a cat can pass his or her head through an opening, the rest of their body easily follows. So now that my head was through, I knew my body would fit as well.

Until it didn't.

And as I experienced a sudden pressure on both sides of my belly, I discovered that no, I could not pass through the pet flap, and yes, Brutus and Harriet were probably right, and I had gained a little weight. And now that I came to think of it: I had indeed been coming and going through the kitchen door lately, and not the pet flap. Out of sheer habit, I thought, but now I realized it was probably because I'd been fitting through the flap less and less, and so unconsciously I'd started avoiding the thing.

Yikes!

"Um… A little help here, you guys?" I said now.

And moments later my three friends were all pushing me in the rear end, attempting to squeeze me through, unfortunately to no avail. I was well and truly stuck. And when I tried to backtrack, I discovered that my progress in both directions was hampered by my belly, which seemed to act like a cork in a wine bottle.

"Max, I think you're stuck," Dooley announced, as if I hadn't noticed the same thing myself.

"See?" said Brutus triumphantly. "I told you that Max had gained a lot of weight lately. And I was right."

"It's not weight," I said. "It's my bones that must have gotten bigger. I probably ate too much calcium."

"It's your belly that has gotten bigger, Maxie baby," said Brutus, and I could hear the grin in his voice. "And as far as I know, there are no bones in bellies."

"Aren't there?" asked Dooley. "I didn't know that."

"I probably shouldn't have eaten that last bowl," I said. "But just you wait and see, when that kibble is digested, my belly will go back to normal, and I'll fit through this thing just fine."

"In the meantime, we're all stuck inside the house," Harriet lamented. "And all because you allowed yourself to get fat, Max."

"I'm not fat," I said in measured tones. "I'm just a big cat, that's all. It's genetics."

"Says you," she said, and I could hear the disappointment in her voice.

"If there's anyone who should complain, it's me," I said. "I'm the one who's stuck."

"At least you have fresh air. We'll be forced to breathe this stale indoor air until someone arrives to get you out of there."

And so it was that moments later, when Gran arrived on the scene, and she found me stuck in the door, she said, "I think it's time for you to go to the vet again, Max."

"Odelia already told us she was taking us," I reminded her.

"Yeah, but now it also looks as if you're going back on your diet," she said as she took a firm hold of me under my front paws and pulled. "You're stuck," she finally concluded.

"I know I'm stuck, Gran," I said, with perhaps more heat than I intended.

"Suck in your breath," she advised.

I sucked in my breath, and she pulled again, putting considerable pressure on my poor ribcage.

"You're not budging, Max. Why aren't you budging?"

"I think it's this pet flap," I told her. "I think it must have shrunk. I've heard that wood shrinks, so that's what must have happened."

"This pet flap is made of plastic, Max," said Gran. "And as far as I know plastic doesn't shrink that much. Now let me try something different." And this time she opened the sliding glass door and moments later I could feel her pulling my legs—both of them.

Unfortunately I still wasn't budging.

"Are you actually sucking in your breath?" asked the old lady as she tried pushing now, again to no avail.

"I've been holding my breath for the past five minutes," I grumbled. "If I hold it in much longer I'll probably expire from a lack of oxygen."

"That's not such a bad idea," I heard Brutus say. "A dead weight is easier to displace."

"Not helpful, Brutus," said Gran. "Okay, this isn't working. We probably need a stronger hand than mine." As luck would have it, just then Marge arrived, and when she came upon the embarrassing scene, offered to push while Gran was pulling. Unfortunately, due to a miscommunication, they both ended up pulling, and I now realized for the first time how those witches in medieval times must have felt when they were put on the rack.

"Ouch!" I exclaimed.

"Oh, sorry, Max," said Marge, and gave me a tickle under my chin, which, in spite of the dire circumstances, made me giggle.

"Don't laugh, Max," Gran grumbled. "Sucking in that belly is what you should do. Suck it in as much as you can!"

Easier said than done. It's hard to suck in a belly filled with food. It makes you feel nauseous, and that's what I was starting to experience at that moment. Definite nausea.

"Okay, Marge, you pull and I push, okay? Now, pull!"

And as Marge pulled and Gran pushed, I felt like one of those dolls kids like to play with, and end up removing Barbie's or Ken's head or limbs in the process.

"This isn't working," Marge announced finally as she wiped her brow.

"Oh, I've got an idea," said Gran. "Where does Odelia keep the soap?"

"Under the sink," Marge said, and for a moment both women disappeared indoors.

Dooley, Harriet and Brutus, released from their confinement, walked out to keep me company and provide moral support. Though judging from their eager looks, and the fact that they made themselves comfortable nearby, where they had a good view of the proceedings, it appeared more as if they saw this as one of those terrible car crashes people are so fond of, and were ready to practice their capacity for rubbernecking.

"Don't you worry about a thing, Max," said Harriet. "I'm sure Marge and Gran know what they're doing. Oh, look— here comes the brown soap."

I gave Marge and the bar of brown soap she was holding, along with a bucket filled with water, a look of concern. "You're not actually going to rub me with soap, are you?"

"Just a little, Max," she said.

And as I watched on, both she and Gran began massaging my midsection with a frothy mixture that smelled very soapy indeed.

"Okay, that should be enough," said Gran behind me, as my entire midsection had been turned into a devastated area. "Now push—or pull! Or… push!"

It took a while for the team to coordinate their rescue efforts, but finally they were jiggling me backward and forward once more, like a tug of war, with me in the middle.

"It's not working!" Gran cried finally, as even the redoubtable brown soap couldn't save me from my tricky position.

"Ooh, I've got it!" said Gran. "Oil!"

"No!" I cried.

"Don't worry, Max," said Marge. "We'll wash it out later… with soap."

"I think Max is probably right," said Dooley now. "I think that pet flap must have shrunk. Pet flaps do shrink, you know. It's the wood. It shrinks when it gets hot. Or cold."

"It's not made of wood, Dooley," said Harriet. "It's made of plastic, and plastic doesn't change shape that much— unless it melts, of course."

Dooley stared at the pet flap. "It doesn't look like it's melted."

"If there's anything that's changed shape," said Brutus, who was clearly enjoying himself tremendously, "it's Max. He's become a lot chunkier lately."

"Thanks, Brutus," I grumbled. "That's very kind of you to say."

"You're welcome, buddy."

"I wish I had a camera," said Harriet. "This is pure gold."

"Yeah, if you posted this on YouTube you'd get millions of views," Brutus agreed.

"No pictures, you guys," I said. It's bad enough to be subjected to this kind of ignoble treatment, but I certainly didn't want the footage to end up on the internet, and turn me into a local laughingstock overnight. I might not be the most handsome cat alive, but I have my pride and I have my dignity, just like any other cat.

And then Gran started massaging my belly with oil, and so did Marge. The sticky substance felt very icky to me, and suddenly I was starting to think that going to Vena, and subjecting myself to her treatment, was probably a lot less bad than what I was going through now. I mean, being rubbed with oil is probably one of the worst things you can do to a cat. Can you imagine having to lick half a gallon of oil out of your belly button? Yuck!

"Okay, push, Marge!" Gran cried. "Or pull—no, push!"

"Oh, will you make up your mind already?!" I said.

And so the shoving and the pushing recommenced, and before I knew it, I zipped right out of that pet flap into Marge's arms, and found myself free of restraints once more!

There was loud yipping and shouts of jubilation from the spectators, and as I took a slight bow to accept the applause, I realized I'd lost the bet, and when I glanced into Harriet and Brutus's smiling faces, I said, "Okay, so you were probably right. I did gain a little weight, and I probably should start dieting again."

"It'll be fine, Max," said Marge. "Vena has been experimenting with a revolutionary new method to monitor pets' health, and she's asked us to include you guys in her pilot program, and of course we wholeheartedly agreed."

I eyed her suspiciously now. "What pilot program?"

"Are we going to be pilots?" asked Dooley.

"Not exactly," said Marge with a laugh, as she put her money where her mouth was and started washing off that horrible oil. The treatment wasn't entirely unpleasant, I must say.

"So... what does it involve?" asked Harriet.

Marge smiled. "Just wait and see. I wouldn't want to spoil the surprise." After rinsing me and rubbing me dry with a clean towel, she gently patted me on the head. "Let's just say you'll find it extremely beneficial. And so will you guys," she addressed my friends.

"Why do I have the feeling I'm not going to like this?" said Harriet.

"*W*ith Better Pet Yet Max will never be overweight again."

"Excuse me," I said. "I resent the term overweight. I feel it doesn't apply to me."

But of course no one paid any attention to me whatsoever. The humans all stood gathered around Vena, who was demonstrating her revolutionary new thing, whatever it was.

"So how does it work?" asked Odelia.

"And how much does it cost?" asked Marge, price-conscious as always.

"Does it work for humans, too?" asked Gran, who seemed to see potential in the thing.

"Better Pet Yet is surprisingly reasonably priced," said Vena, "and no, it doesn't work for humans, though I'm sure there is an alternative. And as far as how it works, it's very simple!"

She spoke in her usual hale and hearty tone, as if trying to hail a cab from across the Grand Canyon. Vena is a formidable woman, with a forceful personality and considerable physical strength. When you know she can pull calves from cows and foals from horses without breaking a sweat, you can imagine bending a mere feline to her will is a cinch. In fact I'm not breaking any confidences when I tell you all cats in Hampton Cove are afraid of the woman, for whom the expression 'force of nature' was originally coined.

"Okay, so you put this collar on your pet, or, if you prefer, I can also implant a subcutaneous chip, and both chip and collar are connected with this app on your phone, with a unique access code, which makes the system absolutely safe and hacker-proof!"

I'd heard the words 'subcutaneous' and 'collar' and immediately pricked up my ears.

"What's subcutaneous, Max?" asked Dooley, giving me a look of concern.

"It means this thing goes under your skin," Harriet explained, and shared anxious glances with both me and Brutus.

"I'm not having anything injected in me," said the latter now. "No way. Uh-uh."

"Me neither," said Harriet. "I vehemently protest against this violation of the physical integrity of my body. My body is my temple, and I won't have it ravaged by butchers!"

"So what is Vena going to do with this thing?" asked Dooley.

"As far as I understand, it's some kind of tracker," I said. "But a smart one that measures all kinds of stuff."

"Better Pet Yet measures blood pressure, heart rate, blood sugar level, subcutaneous fat distribution," Vena was rattling on, deep into her sales pitch now. She'd effectively taken off her vet hat and donned her sales rep cap. "In short, a lot of very important data that will give you the full picture of your pet's health in real-time. It also works with a sophisticated monitoring system with a built-in proprietary and frankly revolutionary algorithm that raises the alarm the moment certain conditions are met—certain predetermined triggers like high blood pressure, increased heart rate, diminished lung capacity…"

"So what do we do when that happens?" asked Marge.

"Isn't it obvious?" said Gran. "We call Vena, of course."

Vena smiled. "That's the best part of Better Pet Yet! You don't have to call me—the system calls me! When you get an alert, I get an alert, too—at least when you are a person in good standing and are current with your fees," she added in a rush of words.

"Amazing," said Marge as she nodded her full endorsement of the scheme.

"I just wish this existed for us, too," said Gran. "Imagine having my blood sugar level and my blood pressure automatically monitored without having to go to the doctor."

"You go to the doctor every day, Ma," said Marge.

"No, but see, with this system I wouldn't have to. This thing does everything for me."

"It… doesn't actually work like that," said Vena, the vet in her rearing its head once more.

"I gotta tell Tex," said Gran as she rummaged in her purse for her phone. "He needs to get on board with this thing. And I even got a name for him: Better Pensioners Yet!"

"I'm a little concerned with security and privacy," Odelia said. "How sure are you that these can't be hacked?"

"Better Pet Yet is part of Intended2, the well-known software giant, so you don't need to be concerned with cybersecurity. Intended2 has the best software developers in the world. They wouldn't launch this app if they weren't a hundred percent sure it was safe."

"Intended2?" said Marge with a frown. "Where have I heard that name before?"

"They also created the popular Mokemon universe," said Vena.

"Oh, right," said Marge vaguely. "I'm not much of a gamer."

"Gaming is only one of the many things the company does."

And as our humans discussed the pros and cons of these nifty new and revolutionary trackers, the four of us awaited the verdict with bated breath.

"A tracking collar is better than a subcutaneous chip," said Harriet, "but not by much."

The last time they made us wear a tracking collar had been a minor disaster, as all the cats in Hampton Cove had been provided with the gadgets, and all of a sudden their owners had realized what their precious cats were up to at night: roaming far and free. They hadn't liked it then, and I was pretty sure they wouldn't like it now.

"At least our humans don't mind when we wander off at night," I said.

"Yeah, but still," said Harriet. "I don't like the idea that Vena knows everything about me." She regarded the collars on the veterinarian's desk with a great degree of suspicion. "And who knows what she's not telling us. That thing might be able to listen to our conversations, track our movements, know what we're up to at all times." She shivered. "Doesn't that sound pretty creepy to you guys?"

"There's a word for this thing," said Brutus somberly. "Big brother."

"I didn't know you had a big brother, Brutus," said Dooley. "That must have been a lot of fun growing up. Do you see a lot of him? Where does he live? Does he look like you?"

"He's not just my big brother, Dooley. He's your big brother, too."

"You mean I have a big brother? Cool!"

"Look, all I'm saying is that I don't like this one bit."

21

"I don't like it either," said Harriet.

"Well, I think it's great," said Dooley, providing the voice of dissent. "If Odelia knows how healthy or unhealthy we are, it's a lot easier for her to take care of us. Like with Max's big belly. All that belly fat is floating around in his bloodstream, and that's very bad."

"No need to concern yourself with my belly fat, Dooley," I said stiffly.

"It's not my health I'm worried about," said Brutus. "It's my privacy."

"But you guys!" said Dooley. "They already know everything about us!"

"I don't care," said Harriet. "It's still a new level of creepy."

"Plus, whatever Vena says, I'm sure these things can be hacked," said Brutus.

"What do you think, Max?" asked Harriet.

"Yeah, you haven't said anything," Brutus added.

"Oh, well," I said with a shrug. "I say let's wait and see."

"Always the diplomat," said Brutus with a disgusted gesture of his paw.

"Yeah, just say what you really think, Max," said Harriet.

"I'm skeptical, too, you guys, but until we know what this is all about, I think we need to defer judgment. Like Dooley says, it might be beneficial for our health, if it means Odelia or Marge or Gran will immediately know when something's not right. Or it could be another disaster, like that time they outfitted us with tracking collars. Too soon to tell."

"Okay, so if your big brother is also my big brother," said Dooley, who'd been thinking hard, "that means you and me are brothers, Brutus. Which means we're family!"

"Oh, Dooley," Harriet sighed.

"So did you have a good time?" asked Marge later that evening during dinner.

"Oh, absolutely," said her husband Tex as he pronged a piece of fish and brought it to his mouth. We were sitting out in the backyard, enjoying one of those balmy evenings that are such a blessing. Around the dinner table sat the entire Poole clan, of course, but also Charlene Butterwick, Uncle Alec's girlfriend and also the town mayor, and Scarlett Canyon, Gran's best friend.

"Did you shoot a lot of nice footage, Dad?" asked Odelia as she fed me a piece of that same fish, which I took an appreciative preprandial sniff at to start those gastric juices flowing. Then she stared at me, and before I could stop her, picked up the fish and said, "According to Vena we should limit your intake of animal proteins, Max, and judging by the Better Pet Yet dashboard I'm afraid you've already reached your limit for today."

"But-but-but!" I sputtered. But Odelia was already turning back to her table partners to continue the conversation and paid me no mind. Clearly the discussion was closed!

"I shot a lot of footage," said her dad, "but I have no idea how to access it." He turned to his son-in-law. "Maybe you can help me, buddy. How do I get that footage onto my PC?"

"Can't be that hard, Dad," said Chase, nodding. "I'll give you a hand after dinner."

"So where did you go?" asked Gran.

"Just the park," said Uncle Alec as he buttered a piece of French toast. And as the three men shared a knowing glance, suddenly I had the feeling there was something they weren't telling us. The others hadn't noticed, as they happily prattled on, the conversation now turning to those snazzy new collars we'd all been outfitted with. But since the dinner table no longer held any promise of food for me, I turned away, feeling a little dejected, and slunk onto the porch swing to lick my proverbial wounds and heal my bruised ego.

"You're not getting any more food, Max?" asked Dooley, who'd been snacking on a piece of fish and now took a break.

"No, Odelia says I've reached my protein intake for the day."

"Oh, that's too bad," said my friend. "Do you want some of mine?"

I eagerly stared at the remnants of his meal, but then shook my head. "I'd better not. Odelia is right. I need to watch what I eat." The recent episode of getting stuck in that awful pet flap had rankled, and I didn't want to repeat the experience if I could help it.

"You're absolutely right, Max," said Brutus, who finished eating his share of fish and now released a tiny burp to indicate he'd eaten his fill and didn't want for more.

"Yeah, Max, you definitely have to watch what you eat," said Harriet.

"Easy for you to say," I grumbled. "You can eat as much as you want without gaining a single ounce. I just have to look at food and I'm gaining weight already. It's just not fair."

"It's those big bones of yours, buddy," said Brutus with a nasty grin.

"Ha ha ha," I said. "Very funny, Brutus. You can't imagine what it's like, to have my body constitution. It's not much fun."

"I know, buddy," said Brutus ruefully. "I was just kidding." And he slapped me on the back so hard I almost toppled off the swing. "You know what you should do? Gain muscle, and lose that flab. It's the flab that gives you trouble," he added as he poked me in the belly, and caused ripples to form there. And then, since he seemed to like the effect of his poking, he jiggled my belly for good measure and loudly laughed at the resulting effect.

"Oh, stop it, Brutus," said Harriet. "You're being very mean."

"It's called tough love, sugar bun," said Brutus. "Max needs to change his ways, and with me as his trainer, I can assure you he will."

I looked up at this. "You're going to be my trainer?" I asked.

"Of course, buddy! We're besties. And I wouldn't be much of a friend if I allowed you to continue down this road, would I now? So I'm going to train you, and when I'm through with you, I can promise you this: you'll be in the absolute best shape of your life. Rock-hard pecs, not an ounce of flab on you—in other words: a completely new you!"

"Oh, okay," I said, causing Brutus to give me a distinct look of censure.

"That's not the positive mental attitude I like to see in my trainees, Maxie baby. Tomorrow, bright and early, I'm starting you on your training program. And I'm not taking no for an answer," he added when I opened my mouth to protest. "This is happening."

"Oh, sweet pea," Harriet gushed. "You're a true friend to Max, aren't you?"

"Of course, snuggle bun. I love the big guy, and I want to see him healthy and happy!"

"Look at this," said Odelia, as she held up her phone. "This is Max, see? And this is his heart rate, his blood sugar level, his blood pressure, and see, this is how many steps he's walked today—not enough, I can tell you," she added with a glance in my direction.

I offered her an appropriately contrite look. I had spent a lot of time on the couch. Frankly I'd been feeling a little weak, now that I was limited in what I could eat. Of course it could all be in my head, but I had experienced a definite sort of weakening sensation.

"And what's that?" asked Tex, interested in the new gadget.

"Those are his brainwaves," said Odelia. "It shows you what he's thinking right now."

"That's so cool," said Charlene. "You can tell from this thing what Max is thinking?"

"Well, it's not sophisticated enough yet, but Vena said that Intended2, the company behind Better Pet Yet, in time wants to be able to translate pets' brainwaves into actual speech patterns and thought patterns, so we'll know exactly what they're thinking."

"You mean we won't need your special skill to understand our pets?" asked Scarlett.

"Isn't it great?" said Marge. "Vena said that if this thing works the way it's designed to, we'll all be able to understand our pets, what they need, what they want, what they're telling us. That way when they're in pain, they'll be able to tell us, and we can do something about it."

"This is nothing short of revolutionary," said Tex admiringly.

"I think we should try this out on our patients, Tex," said Gran. "That way we can monitor them twenty-four-seven."

"I don't know," said Tex. "It seems like a nifty device for pets, but humans are a different beast altogether."

"I'd try it if I were you," said Uncle Alec. "It will give you a definite advantage over the competition."

"What competition? I'm pretty much the only doctor in town."

"This is the way of the future, Tex," said Marge. "And I think you should get on board."

"Mh," said the doctor, who didn't look entirely convinced of the collar's benefits.

"Imagine Ida wearing a collar like this," said Gran, referring to Tex's most faithful patient. "You'll know she's sick before she does. And so you'll work in a preventative capacity and head off any diseases before they even have a chance to manifest!"

"No more cancer," said Chase, nodding. "Or heart disease. Sounds good to me, Dad."

Tex shrugged. "Sounds like a lot of maybes."

"Nothing maybe about it," said Gran. "You better get on board this train, Tex, or else someone else will, and you'll be left behind."

"I think I'd want to outfit my boyfriend with this," said Scarlett. "If I can read his mind I'll know when he's thinking about another woman and then I can dump his ass before he jumps into bed with her." She gestured to Odelia. "Sign me up for one, hon."

Odelia laughed. "This is designed for pets, Scarlett—not boyfriends."

"So? A boyfriend is a pet, right? Not as loyal, obviously, but still a lot of fun."

Once more the three men at the table shared a look of

significance, and I wondered what this was all about. Clearly they were up to something, but what?

But since I had more important things to worry about, namely this ridiculous diet Vena had put me on, and whether I'd ever be able to fit through the pet flap again, I decided not to bother. If they wanted to be secretive, it was their right. In a world dominated by Better Pet Yet, Marge, Charlene and Odelia would know exactly what their men were thinking, by interpreting their brainwaves, and frankly it wasn't the kind of world I wanted to live in. The sanctity of my brain-waves is important to me, you see. At least I think it is. I've never actually looked into what my brainwaves are all about. Maybe there's nothing special about them. Maybe they just show a big image of a nice juicy fish filet or a healthy portion of chicken kibble, and now that I wasn't getting it, I was upset!

4

*T*hat night the four of us were the talk of cat choir. With our cool new collars every single member of the choir wanted to know where they came from, what they did, and where, after we'd explained the ins and outs of the high-tech gadgets, they could get their paws on one.

I wasn't so sure any pet would want one, but clearly the notion of being monitored every minute of every day didn't seem to scare off our friends. They saw the benefits and weren't too worried about the disadvantages or even the blatant violation of their privacy.

"I think it's amazing," Shanille announced, cat choir's director. "Father Reilly knowing what's wrong with me would be so great. Like when I have a headache or something."

"Do you have a headache?" asked Dooley, interested.

"Well, not right now, Dooley, but I get headaches from time to time, sure. Don't we all?"

Dooley stared at her, as if the very notion of headaches was alien to him.

"I don't know," I said. "I'm not sure I want Odelia to know more about what's going on with me than I do."

"No, but see, Max, that's your problem right there," said Kingman, one of my oldest friends. "You need to look at the bright side here. Take cancer for instance."

"Cancer!" said Dooley, as he glanced up at Shanille. "Oh, no, Shanille. That's probably why you have headaches all the time—you have a brain tumor!"

"I don't have headaches all the time, Dooley," said Shanille, slightly annoyed.

"Nobody's got cancer, Dooley," said Kingman, who's an even more voluminous cat than me. "But imagine one of us did. How would you know? You wouldn't, would you? But if we had these collars, Wilbur or Father Reilly would immediately get some kind of alert or whatever—I'm imagining something would start beeping like crazy and the screen would go all red and blinky, like in the movies when the bad guys are launching a rocket to evaporate the free world and James Bond has to stop it, only using a Swiss Army knife and his funny accent. And they'd take us to Vena and she could nip that cancer in the bud."

"I'm not sure this thing picks up tumors," I said dubiously. As far as I had understood Vena, it only monitored my heart-beat and blood pressure and such. It wasn't exactly a panacea for everything that ails us, no matter how well-rehearsed Vena's sales pitch had sounded. But obviously the idea that it could predict cancer appealed to my friends.

"Just look at Buster," said Shanille, as she shook her head.

"Buster has cancer?" said Dooley, alarmed. "Oh, no! How long does he have to live?"

"Buster does not have cancer," said Shanille, "but he does have a cold. And if Fido had kept the door of his hair salon shut and not subjected Buster to that nasty draft, he wouldn't have had to miss cat choir and I wouldn't had to do without my best tenor."

Cat choir is sacred in Shanille's eyes, and anything that impedes its unobstructed and smooth performance on a nightly basis is always a big issue in her view.

"Look, I'm not sure this thing is as sophisticated as it says on the box," I said, trying to counter some of the erroneous notions that were floating around about this device.

"And I think it is," said Kingman. "In fact I think Better Pet Yet is the future, you guys. And I just wish I could talk to Wilbur, for if he gets in at the ground level, I'm sure he'd clean up. What did you say the name of this company was?"

"Um… Intended2," I said. "I think it's Japanese."

"Intended2," said Kingman thoughtfully. "Are they on the Nasdaq?"

"I have absolutely no idea."

He gave me a keen look. "Could you tell your gran to talk to Wilbur and advise him to buy some of their stock? Imagine if you bought Apple or Amazon or Google when they were just starting out, you'd be a gazillionaire now. And the same goes for Intended2."

"I'll tell her," I said, "but I'm not sure—"

"Thanks, Max," he said as he patted my back. Then he eyed my belly affectionately. "So I heard you got stuck in your pet flap?"

I frowned at Brutus, who was chatting with some of our other cat choir friends. "Who told you?" I asked frostily.

"Never mind who told me—is it true?"

I reluctantly admitted that I had, indeed, had an incident involving our pet flap.

"You know what you should do?" said Kingman, and I could tell that he was on the verge of dispensing with some advice.

"What?" I asked wearily.

Kingman's advice, though often well-meant, often makes me feel even worse about my big bones.

"You should ask your humans to make that pet flap bigger," he said. He spread his paws. "Do you see me getting stuck in pet flaps? No, sirree."

I must say that the idea of not having to go on a diet very much appealed to me.

"You mean I should simply ask Odelia…"

"To make it bigger! Make it plus-sized!"

"I'm not sure if that's such a good idea," I said, even as I was thinking that this was probably the best idea I'd heard all day, nay, the best idea I'd heard *ever*—bar none!

"Look, why torture yourself, Max? You just have to accept that you are a plus-sized cat, and act accordingly."

"I'm not plus-sized, Kingman," I said, feeling a little annoyed that Kingman, who's probably twice as big as me, would consider me part of the plus-sized club.

"See, that's your problem right there," Kingman said, nodding. "Denial."

"I'm not in denial. I just don't think I'm plus-sized, that's all."

"Yes, you are, and the sooner you accept the truth the better you'll feel. You are a large cat, Max, just like me, and in fact you're only at the start of your journey." He patted his large belly. "Just look at me—I'm your future, Max—something for you to aspire to."

I looked at him, and frankly I did see my future, and it scared me!

"Do I look unhealthy to you?" asked the large cat.

"Um…"

"I just had my annual checkup last week, and Vena gave me a clean bill of health."

I frowned at him. "She did?"

"Sure! And that's because I am healthy, bud. It all comes down to the same thing." He tapped his noggin. "A positive mental attitude. You have to think yourself healthy, that's all there is to it."

It was the second time that day that someone had mentioned my mental attitude, and I was starting to think there was something in it. I do have a tendency to fret, you know, especially when Odelia gives me a nice piece of fish and then takes it away again.

Still, I had the distinct impression that no matter how hard I tried to think positive, I still wouldn't fit through that dreaded pet flap any time soon.

"I think Kingman is right, Max," said Dooley. "It's all in your mind. If you think you can fit through that pet flap, you will."

"I'm not convinced that's true, Dooley," I said.

"Oh, but it is. I once saw a documentary about three men who believed in thinking themselves to health, and it worked out just fine for them. Of course they all died at the end, but that had nothing to do with the program."

"They all died at the end?" I asked, not finding that a very comforting thought.

"Yeah, see, one suffered from diabetes, the second had a bad heart, and the third had cancer. They didn't believe in doctors, so instead they thought themselves to health."

"Clearly that didn't work."

"Oh, but it did. They got healthier every day in every way, until they died. One of them had a blackout while driving his car and drove into a ravine, his friend's heart stopped in his sleep, which can happen to anyone, and the third ate a bad burger and dropped dead."

Kingman was frowning. "There are no bad burgers, Dooley. Take it from one who knows."

Frankly I found all this talk of health and positive mental

attitudes a little discouraging, but when I expressed this view, both Kingman and Dooley accused me of harboring a negative mental attitude, so I decided to keep my mouth shut and enjoy cat choir rehearsal, which, after all, is the whole point of getting together of an evening in the park with our friends and singing our hearts out. Before we assumed our respective positions, Kingman said he had one more piece of advice for me, and it concerned a few adjustments his human Wilbur had made to his pet flap. I was eager to hear his advice, of course, but then Shanille raised her head and held up her paws as a clear sign that we were about to start, and unfortunately she doesn't allow idle chatter during practice.

And as we all launched into a moving rendition of Céline Dion's *My Heart Will Go On*, with Harriet providing the solo soprano part and going for those hard-to-reach high notes Céline does so well, I couldn't help but think that this idea Kingman had suggested of simply widening the pet flap held the solution to all of my problems: it would make my diet go away, and maybe it would also convince Odelia to drop this tracking collar. For in spite of the fact that I'd professed to the others that I didn't mind that Odelia looked at my brain-waves and whatnot, it still felt a little odd to me that she would be hovering over her tablet or phone at that very moment, studying what was going on inside my brain.

And so when the first shoe of the evening came zipping through the air and found its mark in Tigger, the plumber's cat—humans very rarely display the kind of appreciation for true art that you'd expect them to—I found myself wondering what would happen if someone other than Odelia could read my brainwaves. Not that that was possible, of course, since Vena had assured us that the Better Pet Yet products were absolutely hacker-proof. But still, a tiny part of my brain couldn't help but consider the consequences of just such a contingency.

It just goes to show how this whole pet flap business had weakened my natural positive mental attitude, as Kingman or Brutus would say. I'd quickly gone from being a confirmed optimist to being a weary pessimist!

5

The next morning, I took one look at that pet flap, wondered if I should try squeezing through it again, but decided against it. The ordeal of being rubbed in oil still was fresh in my mind, and I didn't think I could go through it again so soon after the first time.

So instead I passed through the open kitchen door instead. Last night Odelia had been so kind to leave the door open as well, and maybe from now on she always would. Though maybe that was not such a good idea. For even though Hampton Cove is a fairly safe town in many respects, leaving the back door open because one of your cats is too large to squeeze through the pet flap probably is simply ridiculous.

And I'd just emerged into the backyard and was gratefully stretching myself, when the doorbell chimed and immediately I returned indoors to see who it was. I must confess I wasn't in the best mood imaginable, since I'd found my bowl only half full that morning, same as I had found it last night, and it was obvious that Odelia was rationing me. Of course I could have eaten Dooley's share, and I must admit I felt very tempted, but through an act of sheer willpower I refrained from doing so. I'm not the kind of cat who steals food from his friends. That's where I draw the line.

Odelia came down, dressed in skinny jeans and a T-shirt that proudly announced she loved cats, which is certainly true, and called out, "Chase! Are you expecting anyone?"

From upstairs, Chase called back, "No, babe."

"Maybe it's Bambi," I said, referring to our mailwoman Bambi Wiggins. I'd assumed a watchful position in front of the door, and next to me, Dooley had assumed the same position. It's not only dogs who like to watch the postperson arrive, you know, though cats usually refrain from taking a big bite out of their ankles if they can help it.

It wasn't Bambi but a very nicely dressed man. He was in a suit and tie and looked more like a banker or a businessman. Or a lawyer. And it was the latter category he professed himself to fit into, which became clear when he announced, "Sam Goldwyn. I represent George Calhoun. This is the residence of Tex Poole, MD?"

"Um, no, Tex is my dad, actually," said Odelia. "He lives next door. What's this about?"

The lawyer frowned, as he didn't seem to enjoy the notion of being wrong, glanced over to the house indicated, then said, "Apologies for the intrusion—my mistake." And without further ado, excused himself and was gone.

"Odd," said Odelia as she stared after the man, then looked down at the card he'd offered her. "George Calhoun's lawyer? What does he want with dad?"

"Who was it, babe?" asked Chase as he came tramping down the stairs.

"George Calhoun's lawyer," said Odelia, handing Chase the card. "He was looking for my dad."

Suddenly Chase went very quiet. And if I wasn't mistaken

a guilty look crossed his face, as if the unexpected visit of this lawyer wasn't as unexpected to him as it was to us.

"Maybe we better go and take a look next door," he now announced and immediately and without awaiting Odelia's reply, moved out the back door and set foot for the opening in the hedge between our backyard and Tex and Marge's, then disappeared thither.

Odelia frowned after her husband, then glanced down at Dooley and myself, and said, "Do you guys also get the impression something is going on and nobody is telling us what it is?"

"I definitely get the impression Chase knows what's going on," I agreed.

"I think George Calhoun probably wants to hire Tex to play a part in his next movie," said Dooley. "And I think he's right. Tex is going to be a movie star. He's got that look."

"What look?" asked Odelia.

"The look of a leading man," said Dooley. "He could be the next George Clooney."

We pranced along in our human's wake, who was prancing along in her husband's wake, even though prancing is maybe not the term I should use. It was more a sort of thoughtful gait, as if she was thinking about recent events and wondering what was going on.

We arrived next door, and immediately and without further ado moved inside, where we discovered that George Calhoun's lawyer had already entered the house and was in discussion with Tex and Marge, looked upon by Harriet and Brutus, and of course Gran, who never misses a moment when something exciting is going on. And the arrival of George Calhoun's lawyer definitely qualified as the sort of excitement she revels in.

We were gathered in the living room, where the humans had taken a seat at the table, with Gran ensconced on the couch, where she'd been engaged in taking in *Good Morning America*, which she'd just muted to follow what this tough-looking lawyer had to say.

"I would like to advise you of your legal obligation to hand over the footage you illegally shot of my client, Mr. Poole," said the lawyer now, and placed a very thick sheaf of documents on the table in front of an astonished-looking Tex. "And I also would advise you to sign this non-disclosure agreement, prohibiting you from discussing this incident with anyone. Failure to comply will result in damage claims amounting to the sum of one million dollars. You, too, ma'am," said the lawyer, addressing Marge, who just sat there staring at the man. "I am correct in assuming that you are the owner of the drone that illegally captured imagery of my client, am I not?" said the lawyer, when he became aware of a lot of dropped jaws around the living room table, and even dropped cat jaws, too.

"Um..." said Tex, darting a helpless look at Chase, who stood at his right shoulder, like a guardian angel advising him of his rights, perhaps urging him to negotiate a better deal.

"I don't understand," said Marge finally. "What's this all about, Mr. Goldwyn, sir?"

"Your husband flew his drone over my client's property yesterday," said the lawyer, looking as if he was used to having to explain complicated legal matters to laypersons and had resigned himself to this. "As he did, he shot footage of my client engaged in activities that are of a private and highly sensitive nature, and so now my client would like to see that footage destroyed and all those involved in the incident to sign this NDA, barring them from discussing this matter with anyone." He gave Marge a stilted smile. "Though I sense that your husband hasn't yet discussed his unlawful behavior with you, Mrs. Poole."

Marge turned to her husband. "Tex? Is it true what this man is saying? Did you fly that drone of yours over George Calhoun's backyard?"

"Um…" Tex prevaricated, lest he compromise himself legally, and once again glanced up at Chase, the latter having placed a sizable hand on the doctor's shoulder.

In a deep rumbling voice the cop now spoke for the first time. "I'd advise you not to sign this, Dad."

"Are you Mr. Poole's lawyer, sir?" asked the lawyer suspiciously.

"No, I'm a cop, and I don't think it's any of your concern what Tex did or didn't do yesterday."

"Why do you think my husband filmed George doing whatever?" asked Marge, eager to get to the bottom of this thing.

"Because it has reached my client's ear that he did," said the lawyer curtly. He eyed Tex sharply. "If you don't sign this NDA and if you refuse to hand over that drone footage, I will be forced to take this matter further, Mr. Poole. And I can promise you it won't be pretty."

Chase scoffed, "What are you going to do? Go to the police?"

The lawyer sized up Chase. "Being a cop yourself, I can see how you would find this amusing. All the more because your boss, Alec Lip, is not only chief of police, but also the third member of the party involved in this incident. So trust me when I tell you that we won't go to him, or to you, to find legal satisfaction. And we will find legal satisfaction."

"So who are you going to go to?" asked Tex as he cleared his throat.

Mr. Goldwyn gave him a smile that didn't reach his cold eyes. "I'm not going to discuss my strategy with you, Mr. Poole. Will you hand over the footage and sign the NDA or not?"

"Um..." said Tex, this time directing a searching look at his wife, who was frowning and trying to read the document on the table, which presumably was drawn up in the kind of legalese that is very hard for the layperson to decipher.

"Fine," said the lawyer finally, tucking away a very expensive-looking fountain pen. "I will advise my client of your decision not to cooperate. I hope you have a good lawyer, Mr. Poole. Because you will need it." And with these words, he nodded in greeting to Marge, then left without another word.

And as we all sat there, wondering what had just happened, finally Gran said, "What the hell did you do, Tex!"

6

"It wasn't my fault!" were the first words out of Tex's mouth.

"Oh, dear," said Marge as she sank back in her chair.

"The words of a guilty man," said Gran.

"It was my drone. I haven't completely figured out how to work it, so when it flew over George Calhoun's property and shot that footage…"

"What footage?" asked Marge. "What's so special about this footage?"

"That's what I'd like to know," said Gran. "Must be something pretty hot."

"Footage of George Calhoun in intimate embrace with a person who isn't his wife," said Chase in a low voice, apprising all those present of the facts pertaining to the case.

Jaws dropped even more now, followed by startled cries, and a guffaw from Gran.

"George was boning some broad who wasn't his wife?" she cried. "That's classic!"

"It's very embarrassing," said Tex. "I for one wish I'd never laid eyes on the man doing… what it was he was doing."

"And you still have that footage?" asked Gran.

"I have it in my possession," the doctor confirmed.

"I helped Tex transfer it from his drone to his computer," Chase clarified, "and then onto a USB stick, which is now safely tucked away in your upstairs safe, Mom."

Marge frowned. She didn't seem to appreciate all this happening under her nose, so to speak.

"Can I see it?" asked Gran as she eagerly licked her lips. *Good Morning America* clearly had lost its appeal. Who needs celebrities on TV when you can watch the real deal on your son-in-law's drone footage instead?

"No, you can't," said Tex.

"You need to erase that footage, and you need to sign this NDA," Marge said, referring to the voluminous document the lawyer had left behind. "Otherwise they're going to sue us, Tex. You heard what that man said. George Calhoun will sue us for a million dollars!"

"No, he won't," said Chase. "No way is that guy going to sue over footage nobody knows about. For one thing, I'm pretty sure he doesn't want his wife to find out, and when he goes to court, that's exactly what will happen. Her and the rest of the world."

"Oh, dear," said Marge as she brought a distraught hand to her face. "I really don't like this, Tex. Can't you simply delete everything and be done with it?"

"I wanted to delete it," said Tex, "but Chase told me not to, and so did your brother."

"But why?" asked Marge.

"Yeah, why would you tell Dad to keep that footage?" asked Odelia.

"As a precaution to protect us against this exact thing," said Chase, tapping his finger on the thick NDA. "If George sends his lawyer after us, the only thing standing between us and a lawsuit is that film. As long as we have that, George won't dare to come after us. So I suggest you keep that USB stick in your safe, and make sure nobody knows it's there."

"I wonder how George found out about you," said Gran with a thoughtful frown.

"He didn't find out from me," said Tex. "I didn't tell a living soul."

"That's true enough," said Marge, looking mildly hurt. "Why didn't you tell me?"

"Oh, honey, I didn't want you to worry," said Tex, patting his wife's hand.

But she pulled her hand away and folded her arms in front of her chest. "I still don't understand what you were doing flying your drone over George's house," she said now.

"I told you, honey. I have no idea how to control that thing, and it just flew wherever."

"It was Tex's maiden voyage," said Chase, "and he wasn't in complete control of his drone yet." He shrugged his large shoulders. "It could have happened to anyone."

"Yeah, but it happened to you," said Marge with gentle reproach.

"What's going on, Max?" asked Dooley.

"Well, it looks as if Tex accidentally shot some footage of George Calhoun having... relations with a woman who is not his wife."

"Oh," said my friend as he processed this, then: "You mean they were kissing?"

"Yes, Dooley, they were kissing. Kissing a lot."

"That's not very nice of George, Max. If there's anyone he should be kissing it's his wife, not another woman."

"I know, Dooley, and that's exactly why he sent a lawyer to destroy the evidence of what he did."

"Look, I don't know how George found out," said Chase, "but this probably won't be the end of this sordid business. We all know that guys like him are used to getting what they want. So you better keep that USB stick safely tucked away, for when he comes back."

"I don't like this, Tex," said Marge. "We haven't even paid off the new kitchen."

"I don't like it either, honey," said Tex. "But what's done is done."

"It'll be fine," said Chase. "There's nothing George can do as long as we have that video. That's our trump card. It will protect us from any legal repercussions." He squeezed his father-in-law's shoulder gently. "Everything will be just fine, Daddy. Trust me."

Tex winced a little at this endearment. Even though he loved his son-in-law deeply, and thoroughly approved of Odelia's choice of husband, he still wasn't used to the latter calling him Dad or Daddy.

"Uh-oh," said Dooley.

"What is it, Dooley?" I asked.

"Whenever someone in a movie says 'trust me, everything will be just fine,' that's usually when things start going terribly wrong."

"This isn't a movie, Dooley," Brutus pointed out.

"Yeah, when Chase says it'll be fine, it will be fine," Harriet chimed in.

Dooley looked to me for the final word on the matter, but honestly? I had a feeling he was right on the money. This wasn't over yet. Not by a long shot.

eorge Calhoun had realized he was in something of a pickle the moment he spotted that drone flying overhead. But he hadn't fully appreciated the scope of the pickle until his cook had returned from her grocery run that morning and had announced that her master's love life was suddenly the talk of the town. She said the owner of the General Store had been cracking jokes about George's frivolous ways until she'd felt compelled to put the man in his place. But then he'd revealed that actual footage existed— footage captured in full-HD clarity of his infidelity, and if she wanted to, he could get the footage and show it to her. She'd told the man to go to hell, of course, at which point he'd grabbed his phone and had shown her the telephone number of a friend of his who could easily get her hands on that footage. Her name was Vesta Muffin, and she was the mother-in-law of the drone owner, a man named Tex Poole. It was at that moment that George had decided to call his bloodhound lawyer, the one who'd gotten him out of another recent pickle, that time when he'd made a movie criticizing the Saudis, who'd promptly invited him for a visit to their embassy. That's when Sam Goldwyn had warned him that the Saudis had the unfortunate habit of chopping people up into tiny little pieces, never to be seen or heard from again. It was their way of handling folks who weren't enamored with their regime.

The lawyer thusly dispatched, the man had easily acquired the information needed, and had soon learned that Tex Poole had purchased the drone, and had flown it along with his brother-in-law Alec Lip, local chief of police, and Chase Kingsley, local cop.

And George was just checking his sizable fridge to find something to eat—he was big on stress eating—when his telephone chimed and he recognized the ringtone as that assigned to Sam—appropriately it was the Ally McBeal theme song—and he immediately picked up. "Sam," he said as he grabbed some cold chicken and took a tentative sniff.

"No dice, George," said Sam. "I'm afraid they've decided to circle the wagons and play hardball."

"They have, huh? That was probably to be expected. How much did you offer them?"

"Nothing so far. I thought I'd start with the stick before I bring out the carrot. But they're not budging. It's that cop, that Kingsley. He advised his father-in-law to stand firm, and the sap went for it. I think if it was just Poole, he would have folded like a wet blanket."

"How much does he want, this cop?"

"Like I said, I haven't offered them any money. Yet. Thought I'd run it by you first."

"Mh-mh," he said as he bit off a piece of chicken, earning himself a skeptical look from his cook, the wonderful Mrs. Maisel. He gave her a little wave, then walked out onto the patio, wanting to get away from Mrs. Maisel's keen eyes and even keener ears. "Are you sure you got the right guy, Sam?"

"Oh, absolutely. You should have seen this guy Tex Poole's

face. Had guilt written all over it. And his wife and daughter didn't look too happy either."

"God, Sam. Did you have to drag the entire family into this thing? I thought we agreed discretion is paramount here?"

"I know, but what could I do, George? The moment I walked into the place, the whole family came flocking to. Like a scene from The Waltons or something. Even the old grandma was there, on her couch watching breakfast television."

"The grandma?"

"Yeah, some little old lady—spitting image of Estelle Getty."

"Christ."

"Yeah. So what's my limit? How high can I go?"

"One million," he said resolutely.

"Jesus, George, are you sure?"

"Absolutely. Can you imagine what would happen if this got out? My marriage would be on the rocks, for sure, and I'd be the laughingstock of the whole world. Anna would bleed me dry, and take the twins. No, Sam, we need to get on top of this thing. Kill it dead. Destroy that footage before it leaks to TMZ or the National Enquirer."

"I know, and I'm on it, George."

The moment he'd disconnected, he wondered if Sam was the right guy for the job. Obviously Tex Poole was a pushover, and it was in fact the cop who was playing hardball. So they needed to bring him onside pronto, him and that other cop, that Alec Lip. And the best way to get to a man is through his woman. Which meant Poole's wife. And Kingsley's. And as he brought his phone to his ear again, a plan was already forming in his mind.

His next move thusly arranged, he walked back into the house, and was surprised to find his wife waiting there for him. "Oh, hey, sweetheart," he said, and approached her to press a loving kiss to her lips. But she turned her face away from him, a clear sign of trouble. "What's wrong?" he asked, his heart sinking. Could she have found out already?

"You know what's wrong, George," said Anna. She wasn't just a highly successful barrister but also the most gorgeous woman he'd ever met. Unfortunately she could also be tough —probably a consequence or even a necessity in her line of work. When you habitually go after mass murderers in court, you can't help but develop a thick skin.

"Is it the twins?" he asked innocently.

She turned back to him, her eyes blazing with the kind of icy fire many a judge had been on the receiving end of. "You know very well what this is about. That woman!"

He swallowed. "What woman?" he asked, his voice a little hoarse now.

"I just happened to overhear a conversation between the two Olgas upstairs. They were talking about a rumor that's been flying around, about you and that Tammy Freiheit from next door."

He laughed what he hoped was a sufficiently incredulous laugh. When you're an actor, these things come naturally to you, and he liked to use all the tricks in his method acting book to lay it on thick. "Honey, you know what the Olgas are like. They believe everything they read on those online gossip sites. And you know the gutter press hates my guts."

She softened, a clear sign that all she'd heard was foul gossip and nothing solid.

He decided to move in for the kill. "Look, I've been famous for thirty years, and you know how many women I've been linked to in that time? Thousands upon thousands."

"So it's just gossip? You're not involved with that obnoxious Tammy woman?"

"Of course not!" he said, laughing at the sheer ridiculousness of the suggestion. "Why would I care about Tammy Freiheit when I've got you, the mother of my kids?"

"I hate that Tammy. With her inflated chest and puffed-up lips. She's so vulgar."

"I know, honey, I know," he said, tentatively moving in for a hug. This time she allowed him to envelop her in his arms. "Don't let the Olgas get to you. They just love to gossip."

"If they weren't so good at their job I'd let them go," she said, snuggling against his chest.

"If you're going to get rid of every person who gossips about us, there won't be anyone left."

"When are we going back to England, George? I hate how they treat you here."

"Those tabloids you've got back in England are nothing to be sniffed at either."

"I know, but they're nothing compared to the people in this town. It's almost as if they live to gossip. It's just terrible."

"What do you expect? They lead boring, humdrum lives. The only thing they've got is reading those terrible magazines and spreading gossip about celebrities. And like it or not, you married an A-lister, honey."

She glanced up at him, and he pressed a loving kiss to her smooth brow. The ice in those big brown eyes of hers had melted. "I knew what I was getting into when I married you, but it still never fails to amaze me how vicious people can be."

"Just do like me: ignore them and move on."

"Do you promise me there's nothing going on between you and Tammy, George?"

"I promise," he said easily. "On the heads of the twins, Tammy means nothing to me—absolutely nothing."

"Good," she said. "Better keep it that way. Cause if I find out you've been lying, there will be hell to pay."

Once more he swallowed away a slight lump even as that loving, reassuring smile remained firmly in place. He hoped Chuck would come through for him. If Chuck couldn't get his hands on that footage, no one could.

8

Marge was late. This whole business with the lawyer had set her back at least an hour. It wasn't a big deal, since she only needed to open the library at noon today, but she'd hoped to put in some shopping, and now if she didn't hurry, she wouldn't make it on time.

She hated to be late, and prided herself on always being punctual. In all the years she'd been in charge of the Hampton Cove library, not once had she opened even a minute late.

So she hurried up the stairs and disappeared into the shower cabin for a refreshing shower. She'd already decided not to let this whole George Calhoun business affect her too much. Chase said he'd handle it, and she trusted her son-in-law sufficiently to know that he was a man of his word, and would always do his best to deliver on his promises.

And so she lathered up and rinsed off, and scrubbed and washed until she felt like a new person, clean and invigorated. And when she opened the shower cabin door, for a moment she wondered if her eyes were deceiving her, because through the slight cloud of moisture that hung in the bathroom, she suddenly saw what looked like a naked man in front of her. And not only was this man naked, he also looked very familiar. In fact he looked so familiar she rubbed her eyes for good measure, just to be sure she wasn't seeing things. For this man was none other than... Chuck Crush!

"Hey, Marge," drawled the famous actor, who was naked from the waist up, only dressed in boxers. His torso was something to behold: chiseled chest, glistening sixpack, muscular arms. Michelangelo would have loved this perfect male specimen, and would immediately have made plans to sculpt a David II. A lock of Chuck's blond hair fell across his brow, his blue eyes were fastened on hers, and his lips were curled into that trademark half-smile of his. "Thought I'd drop by and see if I can be of any assistance, ma'am," he said now.

And that's when she realized this wasn't a dream but all too real! And so she screamed, as one does, at the top of her lungs.

Immediately Chuck's smile vanished from his face and he held up his hands. "Hold your horses, lady," he said, as he darted an anxious glance at the door.

"Tex!" she yelled.

"Who's Tex? Your husband? Don't call your husband, Marge," said Chuck plaintively. "We don't need your husband. It's just you and me in here, nice and cozy."

"Get out of my bathroom!" she yelled.

"Look, all I want is to have a nice quiet word with you, Marge," said the hunky actor. "Now is that too much to ask?"

"Get out!" she screamed. "Tex!"

But of course Tex wasn't coming. He'd already left for work, along with Marge's ma.

"A very good friend of mine is in something of a pickle, see," said Chuck, moving back a little, just in case Marge would suddenly attack and come out swinging. "And so he asked me to help him out, and I wouldn't be much of a friend if I didn't at least give it a shot."

A little calmer now, since she didn't have the impression the actor was about to molest her, she wrapped her towel around herself and said, "What the hell are you doing in my bathroom? How did you get in?"

"We don't need to go into all that," said Chuck, affecting his most charming smile, the smile that had earned him a devoted following. Even Marge had to admit she wasn't fully immune to that smile and the man's obvious charm.

She frowned. "Are you really…"

"Chuck Crush at your service, ma'am," he said, extending a hand, then immediately retracting it when her frown deepened. He cleared his throat. "Now, look, this friend of mine, he had his privacy invaded, see."

"Like you're invading my privacy?"

"You've got me there, Marge," he said. "You've got my number." He then turned serious. "Look, all I want is that footage. Hand it over and I'll be out of your hair—which is gorgeous, by the way—do you use conditioner? Don't answer that. Just give me the footage, or the camera or whatever, and we'll consider this chapter closed."

"What footage?" she asked, understanding dawning. Like most people, she enjoyed reading the gossip magazines at the hair salon, and it was a well-known fact that Chuck Crush and George Calhoun had been close friends for years. They'd even made a number of successful movies together, and supported each other through thick and thin. Could it be that George had sent Chuck to retrieve that incriminating footage for him?

"You know what I'm talking about, Marge," said Chuck, eyeing her closely.

"I have no idea what you're talking about," she said, deciding to follow Chase's line in this matter: staunch denial, so they could hold on to that footage and successfully defend themselves against George's attempts to get it back and create legal trouble for them.

"And I think that you know perfectly well what I'm talking about."

"Why aren't you wearing any clothes?" she asked, wondering why he would show up like this.

He glanced down at his perfect physique. "I always walk around like this," he said, as if it was the most natural thing in the world to look like some modern-day Adonis. "Look, are you going to hand over that footage or not?" He quirked a seductive eyebrow in her direction, triggering a minor spasm in her lower abdomen. The sensation wasn't completely disagreeable, she had to admit.

"Like I said, I honestly have no idea what you're talking about," she said, continuing to toe the family line decided upon earlier.

Chuck's smile didn't waver. "Look, if you hand over that footage now, I'll make it worth your while, Marge." He approached her, and placed a hand on her cheek. "You're a very attractive woman, and I happen to be into older women."

That tremor in her lower abdomen turned into a watershed, but she decided that enough was enough. So she slapped him across the face, careful not to lose control of her towel, lest it dropped to the floor, and said, in as harsh a tone as she could muster, "Get out, Chuck, before I call the cops."

Still smiling that seductive smile, he shrugged and said, "Your loss, Marge." But then he did as she demanded, and walked out. But not before saying, "If you change your mind, you'll find that I've put my private number in your phone." And then he was gone.

She blinked a couple of times, wondering if she'd dreamed the scene or if she'd really been visited by Chuck

Crush in her own bathroom, and he'd tried to seduce her in exchange for incriminating footage of his best buddy, the equally famous George Calhoun.

But then she figured the scene had indeed been all too real, and a smile crept up her face. Her hand was still stinging, and she now wondered how many women could say they'd spurned Chuck's advances and had slapped him across the handsome face.

Probably not too many!

But then she was strong again, and decided she probably needed to tell Chase that his plan had sprung a leak. If George was prepared to send in Chuck, what else was he prepared to do to lay his hands on that footage!

9

I was staring at the pet flap and thinking about what Kingman had told me last night when Dooley joined me.

"What are you doing, Max?" he asked.

"I'm wondering who to ask about a carpentry job," I said.

"You should ask Tex. He loves that kind of thing."

"I know he does, but he's also very bad at it."

"Why do you need a carpenter, Max?"

"Because I want this pet flap made bigger."

"Oh, you want to be able to pass through it again?"

"Yes, Dooley. I want to be able to pass through it whenever I want, and not having to go on a diet every time I get stuck in the darn thing."

"You could ask Gran. I'm sure she knows a carpenter. If you ask Marge or Odelia, they'll just tell you to lose weight, but Gran will understand. She's more understanding that way."

I smiled. It was exactly the line of thinking I'd been following myself. Odelia is probably the best human on the planet, but she can be a little staunch in her views, especially where things like health or weight are concerned. Odelia is a fitness fanatic, you see, and so is her husband. They go to the gym all the time, and both look like paragons of health and fitness. Chase looks as if he could compete in the Mr. Universe competition, and Odelia probably has the lowest body mass index in town. Unfortunately they're saddled with a cat who's not a fitness fanatic at all. Even though I don't mind being healthy, I also like my regular intake of food, and even though I walk around a lot, I'm not into fitness myself. Too much trouble. And also, I hate exercise. It makes me cranky.

"You know, I thought I heard Marge screaming just now," said Dooley.

"Screaming? What do you mean?"

"Well, I was trying out some of that new kibble she got us? And I heard her screaming for Tex. And then I saw a naked man walk down the stairs and out the door."

I blinked and slowly transferred my gaze from that pet flap to my friend. "A naked man?"

"Yes, and he looked familiar, too. I'm pretty sure I've seen him in a movie."

"Let's go," I said curtly. It was clear to me now that Marge needed our help—fast!

And so we made our way into the backyard of Marge and Tex, then into the house—not through the pet flap, since it has the exact same size as Odelia's pet flap, unfortunately, but through the kitchen door—and as we went in search of Marge, we found her in the kitchen, looking refreshed and with a smile on her face and humming a pleasant tune. If she'd been assaulted by a naked actor she certainly didn't look it.

"Are you all right, Marge?" I asked, concerned in spite of her merry appearance.

"Oh, absolutely," she said as she gave me a happy smile. "Something extraordinary happened to me just now, Max."

"Yeah, Dooley told me."

"Did the naked man hurt you, Marge?" asked my friend.

"No, he didn't, Dooley," said Marge.

"What did he want?" I asked.

"He wanted me to hand him George's footage."

"You mean the drone footage?"

Marge nodded as she absentmindedly gazed out the window into the backyard. "Mh-mh," she said. "But of course I told him I didn't have it." She turned to face us. "He's very nice, you know, and he left me his number, in case I changed my mind. Obviously I'm not going to change my mind, but it was very kind of him to try and help out his best friend."

"Who was it?" I asked the million-dollar question.

"Chuck Crush."

"Oh, dear," I said, and immediately saw what must have happened. "George sent him?"

Marge nodded again. She had a blush on her cheeks and she couldn't stop smiling. Which was to be expected, after a close encounter with the naked or semi-naked Chuck Crush. It isn't every day that one of the most famous and attractive actors of his generation decides to drop in on you, asking for a favor.

"So why was he naked?" I asked, wanting to clear up a minor point.

Marge shrugged. "He's used to walking around with his shirt off. I guess he likes it."

"I'm glad he didn't hurt you, Marge," said Dooley. "When I heard you scream I was worried and so I went to get Max."

"I screamed because I was surprised," she said. "But then when I saw that it was Chuck Crush and he didn't seem dangerous, I relaxed." She sighed a wistful sigh. "Chuck Crush." She now emitted a girlish giggle. "Wait till I tell my friends. They're not going to believe me!" And then she picked up her purse from the kitchen table and walked out, without bothering to close the back door.

"She looks happy, Max," said Dooley.

"A little too happy," I said censoriously.

"Do you think Marge is having an affair with Chuck Crush?"

"I doubt it. She might feel a little flustered now, but I doubt whether she'll actually engage in carnal relations with the man."

"She did look very excited," my friend remarked.

"That's because it's a fantasy of many women to get with a movie star, Dooley. But when push comes to shove, I think they'll find it's not all it's cracked up to be. You see, movie stars are also regular people, and just like regular people, they don't always live up to the expectations. Besides, I'm sure Chuck wouldn't take things to such an extreme."

"Not even to help his friend George?"

"Not even to help his friend George."

And then it was our turn to go walkabout. Kingman had never finished telling me about the modifications Wilbur made to his pet flap, and suddenly I was dying to find out.

10

*W*e were walking along in the direction of downtown Hampton Cove when all of a sudden we came upon a group of kids. They seemed to be engaged in some kind of activity on their phones, for they were excitedly gibbering amongst themselves, and glancing intently at their respective devices all the while.

"I think he's here," said one of the kids, a fair-haired girl of about twelve.

"If I find him, I'll have the highest score in town," said a boy, who was even younger than the girl, had freckles all over his face, a bucktooth, and looked as if he still needed his mom to wipe his nose.

"Don't these kids have to be in school, Max?" asked Dooley.

It was the exact same question I'd been asking myself, to be honest.

"Maybe they're on a school trip," I suggested. "Or on some kind of assignment?"

But as we passed, suddenly all of the kids turned in our direction, their faces eager and their expressions fervent, glancing from their phones to us, then back to their phones and finally, all eyes settling on us. Excited murmurs ran through the small group, and all of a sudden the fair-haired girl cried, "It's them! It's MokeMax and MokeDooley!"

"I saw them first!" cried the buck-toothed young boy with the freckles, and as one kid, suddenly they all descended upon us, with the clear intent of catching us!

"Run, Dooley!" I cried when it became clear our lives were in danger. "Run like the wind!"

And so Dooley did exactly as I instructed: he ran like the wind, and soon was at the end of the street, leaving his pursuers far behind. Of course Dooley is a much smaller feline than me, and even though I tried to keep up, and managed to put a distance between myself and my persecutors, I still had a hard time making my getaway. Steve McQueen I certainly am not, nor did I have a Mustang at my disposal. I'm a cat built for comfort, you see, not speed, and also, I have those big bones of mine to contend with, as discussed, whereas Dooley's bones are probably light as a feather, not unlike a bird!

After a while, I was panting and clearly in trouble, and the small group of excited kids was gaining on me!

"I've got him—MokeMax is mine!" said the snot-nosed kid as he reached out to grab me by the neck.

But just then I was lucky enough to spot a tree by the side of the road and zoomed right underneath that tree and disappeared from view, making sure those kids couldn't get at me. And to make sure I was fully out of reach, I even took the precaution of scooting up that same tree, like only cats can, claws digging into bark, and soon was ensconced in the top of that tree, and found myself gazing down at that small group of kids, who were pointing at me, eager to lay their grubby little hands on me!

In the distance, I could see Dooley still going strong,

doing a Forrest Gump and disappearing from view, and then it was just me and those darn kids!

"So now what?" I murmured to myself. I'd well and truly gotten myself into a jam now, hadn't I! And to my extreme distress suddenly the snot-nosed kid started climbing the same tree I was lodged in, and branch by branch crawling closer to where I was sitting! From time to time he stopped to wipe his nose on his sleeve, then continued on.

"Oh, darn it," I said as I watched that horrible kid with an expression of extreme glee on his face move ever closer! "Get lost!" I told him in no uncertain terms as he moved within a couple of yards from me. "Get away from me, you horrible little brat!"

But of course the kid wouldn't listen. He was too busy showing off to his friends, and proving that he was the one who would 'catch MokeMax!' whoever this mysterious MokeMax could be. Obviously the kid had me confused with another creature.

Lucky for me I'm equipped with a nice set of claws, and as he grabbed for me, I gave his hand a nasty scratch, prepared to defend myself with tooth and claw if necessary.

"Ouch!" he said, then yelled to the others, who all stood watching on from down below: "He scratched me! MokeMax just scratched me!"

"Just grab him already, Ralphie!" one of his buddies shouted. "Or no points for you!"

And so it was with renewed fervor that Ralph made a grab for me, pointing with his phone in my direction for some reason, at which point I decided enough was enough, and made the great leap to the nearest house, where I reached the roof with only millimeters to spare, and started licking the claw I'd used to stave off Ralphie's attempts to corner me.

Ralphie wasn't deterred, though, and encouraged by the

baying crowd of kids below, also tried to make the jump to the gutter. Lucky for me Ralphie wasn't built like a cat, so my new hiding place was well out of reach for the horrible kid. Also, and much to my delight, it now appeared as if he was stuck, and didn't dare to get back down!

And so as I watched from the roof of the house, about ten minutes later the fire department arrived, and a fireman was dispatched to get Ralphie out of his predicament.

"This isn't over, MokeMax!" he screamed as he was freed from his position in the top of the tree. He shook his freckled fist at me. "I'll get you next time—just you wait and see!"

"Shut up, kid," said the grumpy fireman, who probably had had to interrupt a great game on television back at the precinct to get this annoying kid out of a tree.

I meowed, hoping the fireman would rescue me from that roof, but apparently that was too much to ask, for he pointedly ignored me, and as I watched, the activity dispersed: the fire truck rode drove off, the kids probably went to school, where they belonged, and then I was alone once more. Except for Dooley, who'd returned, and was staring up at me.

"Max?"

"Dooley!" I said. "Am I glad to see you!"

"Why are you on that roof?"

"I was trying to get away from those horrible kids."

"Can you get down?"

I looked around. There was that nearby tree, of course, but I didn't think I'd be able to get down that way. And then there was the drainpipe, but I was absolutely sure I wouldn't be able to get down that way!

"Looks like I'm stuck," I said sadly.

"Wait there, Max," said my friend. "I'll go and get help!"

I didn't really have much of a choice but to wait there, and so I settled in for the duration, and thought hard thoughts about kids being allowed to wander around unsupervised and harass unsuspecting cats. Isn't there some law about keeping kids on a leash at all times? Or is that dogs? At any rate, I thought the rule should probably apply to both species alike, since both of them are equally annoying to us felines.

It only took Dooley about twenty minutes, but when he returned it was with both Odelia and Chase in tow.

I waved at my humans, and said, "I'm sorry, Odelia, I was chased up here by kids!"

"I know," said Odelia, shielding her eyes as she took in the scene. "Dooley told me all about it. But why were they chasing you?"

"I have no idea!"

"They kept saying they were hunting MokeMax and MokeDooley," said Dooley.

Odelia glanced to her husband, who spat in his hands, and said, "I'll get him down for you, babe—no sweat." And before my astonished gaze, Chase climbed that tree as if he'd never done anything else his entire life! And as he reached me he said, "Now jump, Max. Jump straight into my arms, buddy. Don't be afraid—I'll catch you!"

And so I jumped, and soon was being carried down by Chase, resting peacefully and safely on his broad shoulders, and at that moment my warm and fuzzy feelings for the man Odelia was so clever to select as her mate for life increased with leaps and bounds.

"How many times has Chase saved us, Dooley?" I asked once we were safely on the ground again.

"Must be dozens of times, Max," said Dooley as we gazed adoringly at the tall cop.

"Thanks, Chase," I said. "You're my hero."

"And mine," said Dooley.

"You're my hero, too," said Odelia, and pressed a tender kiss to her husband's lips.

"All in a day's work," said the tall cop as he wiped his hands and dusted his pants.

And as we stood there, suddenly a man materialized, carrying a bulky camera, and said, "Odelia Kingsley?"

"That's me," said Odelia good-naturedly.

"I'll give you ten thousand for it," said the man.

Odelia laughed. "My cats are not for sale."

"Not the cats," said the man, making a face as if she'd offered to feed him a plate of bugs. "The George Calhoun film. I'll give you twenty thousand in cash. Final offer."

She regarded him sternly. "You're a paparazzo, aren't you? I thought I recognized you."

The guy shrugged. "We all gotta make a living. So how about it, Odelia? Are you selling or not?"

"Not," she said. "And besides, I don't even know what you're talking about. What film?"

"Cut the crap, lady," said the guy nastily. "The whole town is abuzz with the story. How your dad managed to fly a drone over Calhoun's pool and caught him in flagrante delicto with some hot babe. This is the story of the year— nay, the decade!"

"I think you better get lost now," said Chase as he took a menacing step forward.

The guy wasn't deterred, though. Your true pap needs more incentive to get lost than a burly cop making threatening noises. "Look, I'm prepared to go as high as fifty thousand. What do you say? You won't get a better offer." His face clouded. "Unless of course George himself has been in touch. How much did he offer to have the film destroyed?"

"Look, I honestly have no idea what you're talking about," said Odelia. "Now please leave us alone."

"I guess you want to keep the scoop for yourself," said the guy as he started following along as we moved in the direction of Chase's car. "I should have known—ace reporter such as yourself. Though I have to admit I didn't think Dan Goory had it in him to print footage like that in the Gazette. Always figured he ran a classy paper, not a gutter rag."

"Will you just get lost?" said Chase as he swiped in the direction of the pap as if he was a pesky fly, which to all intents and purposes he probably was.

The guy shrugged. "Have it your way." But before he walked off, he said, "If I were you I'd think long and hard before I subjected those cats of yours to this Mokemon nonsense, but then of course you're probably doing it for the story, aren't you?" And as he took a couple of snaps of me and Dooley, he added with a chuckle, "It's not just George who's notorious—those cats of yours will soon be the talk of the town, too!"

And then he was mounting his motorcycle, and roared off, leaving us to stare after him, our minds abuzz with questions and not a lot of answers.

11

*O*delia and Chase dropped us off in downtown Hampton Cove, but not before ascertaining that we'd survived our ordeal to their satisfaction.

I assured them I was fine, and so was Dooley, and then both of our humans took off in the direction of their respective offices and Dooley and myself set paw for the General Store, where I still wanted urgent speech with Kingman.

The voluminous cat was holding forth on the sidewalk in front of Wilbur's store as usual, and when we arrived had just said goodbye to two pretty felines, who sashayed off, watched after by an appreciative Kingman. He's an aficionado of the female feline form, and the appreciation is entirely mutual, which never ceases to amaze me, since Kingman is not exactly the Chuck Crush or George Calhoun amongst cats. But then the female mind has always been something of a mystery to me.

"Dooley, Max," he said, never taking his eyes off the disappearing felines' backsides.

"Kingman, last night you started to tell me something, but then we got sidetracked."

"Oh, yeah?" he said, finally dragging his attention away from his female friends and fastening it on yours truly.

"You said something about certain modifications Wilbur made to your pet flap?"

"Oh, that's right. Completely forgot about that. Come on in—it's easier if I show you."

And so we followed him into the shop, past Wilbur, who kept one eye on a football game on his small television and another one on the wares that had been placed on his conveyor belt, past the racks of dried goods and the meat section, several fridges and coolers, and finally through the plastic strip door curtain that acts as a divider between the store and Wilbur and Kingman's home. We finally reached the kitchen, and Kingman halted in front of the back door and what looked like an intricate boxy contraption.

"This is it," Kingman pronounced proudly. "The Pet Funnel 5000. Wilbur got it on the internet."

"But what is it?" I asked curiously as I studied the thing. It had been bolted into the door, was square in shape, and had a number of buttons placed on a control panel.

"It's pretty simple, actually," said Kingman, "though the technology behind it is state-of-the-art. So all I have to do is position myself right in front of that little camera."

"Oh, is that a camera?" asked Dooley, as we both stared at a small round eye.

"A scanner, actually. It scans my face, then searches its database for my likeness, and when it finds me, the little plastic door slides up and I can go through. And the great thing is: it's adjustable. In fact the manufacturer guarantees it adjusts to any pet of any size. Here, let me show you how it works."

And as he proceeded to step in front of the small camera, there was a buzzing sound, and moments later a light blinked green, the transparent plastic door slid up, like the door of a garage, and Kingman walked through. Immediately the door closed again.

"Now you try!" he shouted from the other side of the door.

So I positioned myself in front of that camera, the same buzzing sounds indicated the machine was thinking hard, and then... nothing. All I could see was a tiny red light.

"It doesn't recognize you!" Kingman shouted through the door. "Wilbur has to feed you into the system first or it won't let you pass!" He followed the same procedure and moments later had joined us in the kitchen again. "Pretty nifty, huh?" he said, glowing with pride.

"Pretty nifty," I agreed.

"It's a smart system. It knows who I am, and only allows me to pass through."

"So you can't invite a friend?" asked Dooley, curious.

"No, it only allows the cats Wilbur has decided to grant access. It's designed to make sure no unwanted pets enter the house. Only your own pet is allowed in."

"So what do you do if you want to invite a friend?" Dooley insisted.

"The old-fashioned way," said Kingman. "I make a lot of noise until Wilbur shows up and opens the door."

"Cool," I said. "The things they invent these days, huh?"

"There's a lot more this baby can do," said Kingman. "Imagine for instance that parents don't want their cat or dog to go into the nursery. They can install the Pet Funnel 5000 on the nursery door and program it so it won't allow cats or dogs to go in there."

"Can't they simply close the door and not install the Pet Funnel 5000?" I asked.

He thought about that for a moment. "I guess that's also a possibility," he allowed.

"How big does it get?" asked Dooley, glancing in my

direction. He knew that was the real reason I was interested in this device.

"Like I said, it can go as big as you want. It's totally adjustable. In fact it automatically adapts to the pet that needs to pass through. And if you consider that this thing is designed for any pet, of any size, also big dogs like Dobermans, it's easy to see why this baby has become the go-to pet flap for the modern pet parent."

Like his own pet parent, Kingman was a born salesman. He certainly had sold me!

"I want one!" I said immediately.

"Can a cow pass through the Pet Funnel 5000, Kingman?" asked Dooley.

"No, Dooley. A cow can't pass through the Pet Funnel 5000."

"Can a horse pass through the Pet Funnel 5000?"

"Just tell Odelia to call Wilbur, Max. He'll be able to get her a nice discount."

"Can an elephant pass through the Pet Funnel 5000?"

"By the way, did you hear about that George Calhoun business?" asked Kingman, ignoring Dooley. Then he thunked his head with his paw. "Oh, silly me. Of course you heard. It's Tex who made that video. So where does he keep it? At the house?"

"What does the 5000 stand for, Kingman?" asked Dooley.

"Um…" I said, not sure I felt comfortable discussing the George Calhoun affair with one who's as notorious a gossip as Kingman.

"Look, whatever you do, make sure you keep it somewhere safe," said Kingman now as we traversed the house again, and ended up back in the store, traipsing along the rows of wares. "Cause I overheard a woman talking on the phone this morning, who said she wanted that footage and she was going to get it, too."

"What woman?" I asked with a frown.

"Don't know the name. She comes in here from time to time. Pretty young blonde."

"Doesn't ring a bell," I said.

"Can a dinosaur pass through the Pet Funnel 5000, Kingman?" asked Dooley.

The big cat gave Dooley an indulgent smile, then turned back to me. "Watch your step, Max. I got the impression a lot of people are after that footage, and plenty of them will stop at nothing to get it."

Oh, dear. As if it wasn't enough that I had my weight and pet flap issue to deal with, or pesky kids chasing me up trees, now I had to act as my humans' keeper, too.

"A naked Chuck Crush showed up in Marge's bathroom this morning," Dooley announced as we both lay down next to Kingman, who'd resumed his position in front of the store.

"Chuck Crush?" said Kingman, raising his eyebrows meaningfully. "What did he want?"

"The George Calhoun footage," I said.

"Oh, that's right. George and Chuck are like this," said Kingman, intertwining his claws to indicate how close Chuck and George were. "Well, looks like it's started already."

"And a paparazzo offered Odelia fifty thousand dollars for the film," Dooley continued.

Kingman whistled through his teeth. Yes, cats can whistle, though it's not an easy trick to master. But Kingman, who's a keen whistler, has perfected the technique. Usually he whistles after passing females, but now it was more as an expression of his astonishment. "That's a lot of money. So did she accept?"

"No, she didn't," I said. "She told the paparazzo to get lost."

"If I were her I would have taken the money," said Kingman. He shrugged. "But that's just me, of course. I guess I take after my human in that sense. I just love the money."

We all looked up at Wilbur, who was happily sniffing a hundred-dollar bill before giving it a kiss and tenderly tucking it into his cash register, like one would a baby.

"I don't think they want to give that film to anyone," I said. "They agreed to keep it as a guarantee George won't come after them with his lawyers and take them to court."

"A lawyer showed up at the house this morning," Dooley supplied. "He said he represented George and wanted Tex to hand him the film and sign an NBA."

"NDA," I corrected him.

"Or else he would sue."

"See, that's the trouble with these Hollywood types," said Kingman. "They immediately threaten to sue. That's why you need to get this film out into the open. That way they can't sue."

"I would think that's exactly when they'd sue," I said.

"No, see, the moment that film is out there, you're safe. There's nothing they can do. Of course you don't publish it yourself. You leak it, so it can't be traced back to you."

"Huh," I said, wondering if Kingman was right. It would certainly ease the pressure George was bringing to bear on our humans. First that lawyer, then Chuck Crush and then the paparazzo. If this kept up, soon all of George's friends would descend upon the house to lay their hands on that film.

But since I had other, more pressing matters to consider —namely how to convince Odelia to buy me this Pet Funnel 5000—I soon forgot all about George and his embarrassing film, and gave myself up to thought.

*A*nd I probably would have lain there indefinitely, for I had to admit Kingman had selected a perfect spot to engage in one of cats' favorite activities, namely people watching, if not suddenly I detected that same small group of kids bearing down on us once again, uttering cries of 'MokeMax is close!' and 'This time I'll catch him!'

"Oh, no," I muttered, and tried to hide underneath a crate of fresh tomatoes.

Unfortunately it appeared as if our positions were already compromised, for as the kids approached, they immediately zoomed in on us, making a beeline for me and Dooley.

And so for the second time that morning, I bellowed, "Run, Dooley, run!"

And then we were running for our lives once again. This time I made the tactical decision to head indoors, hoping they wouldn't follow us into the store, but of course those pesky kids defied all reason and the rules of propriety and did exactly that.

Dooley and I raced through the shop, threading our way through the legs of the myriad of customers sampling

Wilbur's fine wares, past the counter where fresh meats and fish are sold, past the fridges filled with dairy products, and into the private space Kingman had shown us only moments before. But judging from the excited chattering from the kids, led by that blond-haired girl and that freckle-faced snotty-nosed kid, that plastic strip door curtain didn't deter them from following us, and neither did the sign that said, 'Private! Keep out!' And then we were faced with a barrier that seemed both inviting and formidable in its refusal to let us pass: the high-tech Pet Funnel 5000!

"It won't let us pass, Max!'" said Dooley, as the thing plainly refused to budge.

The light blinked red, and it even made a tinny beeping sound as if to say: 'You will not pass!' Even Gandalf the Grey could have picked up a thing or two from this machine.

And so we decided to try a different tack, and raced up the staircase, hoping that the kids would at least not follow us there, as it led straight to Wilbur's apartment above the store. They wouldn't dare to go there, would they?

But of course they did!

"I've got 'em!" the snotty kid bellowed.

"We've got 'em cornered!" the blond girl screamed, their phones held out like weapons in front of them, and apparently showing them exactly where to go!

"I don't believe this," I told my friend as we slipped underneath Wilbur's bed in the hope of riding out this storm. "They seem to know exactly where we are at all times!"

"I don't know how they do it, Max," said Dooley, panting hard. "It's almost as if they can smell us!"

Moments later we heard them moving closer, and I could already hear the nasally challenged kid snuffling and whispering, "I think they're under the bed!"

"I saw them first!" said the fair-haired girl. Her and the other kid seemed to be the ringleaders.

75

"They found us, Max!" Dooley cried in utter dismay.

"I know—let's give them the slip—out through the balcony. Now!"

And so we raced from under the bed, and made our way over to Wilbur's bedroom balcony, and glanced around frantically for an avenue of escape. All I could see was another tall tree, and even though I was getting sick and tired of trees, I saw no other recourse than to make the jump, and moments later both Dooley and myself were up another tree, watching as five kids stood crowding on Wilbur's balcony, excitedly pointing their phones, and gibbering that they'd found us and how they were going to catch us!

"I don't get it, Max!" Dooley said. "How do they do it!"

"And more importantly: why!" I returned his heart's cry with a question of my own.

And since the snotty kid seemed eager to make the jump, too, but was held back by the blond girl, and presumably also by the memory of that fireman who'd recently had to save him from that other tree, we climbed as high as we could, straight to the top.

And as we watched on with distinct interest, suddenly Wilbur himself appeared on the scene, and bellowed, "What the hell are you kids doing in my bedroom! Out! Get out now!"

And even though the kids were obviously reluctant to abandon their prey, they adhered to Wilbur's wish to rid his bedroom of five nosey kids by following him out.

And then it was just Dooley and myself again—up there in that tree!

"Now how do we got down from here?" asked Dooley.

"We can always jump back to that balcony," I suggested.

But to do that we first needed to climb down again, and as I have already amply demonstrated, while climbing trees is a cinch for us, climbing down is a lot harder.

And as we sat there in that tree, wondering how to proceed, all of a sudden we saw movement in Wilbur's bedroom again, only this time it wasn't the kids, or Wilbur, but a young blond woman, who reminded me of the blond woman Kingman had described. She was rifling through Wilbur's stuff and glancing back to the door in a way that made me assume she was extremely eager not to be detected by the homeowner himself.

"What is she doing, Max?" asked Dooley, looking on with distinct interest.

"Looks like she's looking for something," I said as I watched her like a hawk.

"Looking for what?" asked my friend.

"Money, maybe?" I said. "Wilbur probably keeps some ready cash at hand."

Many people incorrectly assume that since Wilbur runs his own business, and has a flourishing shop on Main Street, he must be the local Scrooge McDuck, swimming in gold. I very much doubt that is the case, though. Oftentimes your small business owner isn't swimming in gold so much as drowning in bills, and has trouble keeping his head above the water.

As we watched on, the woman now appeared on the balcony, took out her phone, and urgently spoke into the device. "I can't find it, Marky. Are you sure it's here?" She listened for a moment, then grimaced. "I've looked everywhere, and I don't think he's got it." She listened again for a few beats, then said, "Poole? As in Tex Poole, that nice doctor?"

"She's talking about our human, Max!" Dooley said. "She's talking about Tex!"

"I know, Dooley," I said, as I tried to hear what this Marky person was saying. Unfortunately, even though cats have powerful hearing, I couldn't quite catch it.

"Okay, Marky. If you're sure," said the woman, and then disconnected. She stood staring off into space for a few moments, then returned inside, and was gone.

Moments later, Kingman appeared on the balcony, saw us clinging to that tree, and laughed heartily. I guess we did provide a pretty funny sight.

"I better get Wilbur out here," said Kingman. "Unless you want to keep hanging out there all day?"

"No, Kingman," I said. "I don't."

"Me neither," said Dooley in a small voice.

And shaking his head at such merriment, Kingman disappeared, and even though I would have spurred him on in word or deed, it was obvious he wasn't in a hurry to get us out of our predicament!

And so we watched first how Wilbur appeared, who also produced a loud guffaw when he saw us clinging to his tree, then disappeared again. It took another twenty minutes before Odelia and Chase arrived, and Chase, bless his heart, heroically made the jump from balcony to tree, and was soon carrying both Dooley and myself down from there, to return us to terra firma, where Odelia was patiently awaiting the second rescue operation of the day.

"What happened?" she asked once we were safely down again.

"Those darn kids again," I said. "They were chasing us."

"They seem to know exactly where we are all the time," said Dooley.

"They look at their phones and they can pinpoint our location," I added somberly.

"Poor fellas," said Odelia as she crouched down and gave us both a cuddle.

We moved inside, and Chase now washed off some of the bark which had stained his jeans with a rag and some water from Wilbur's sink.

We both glanced up at the heroic cop. "We love you, Chase," said Dooley fervently.

"Yeah, you're the greatest, Chase," I chimed in.

"I don't know what's going on," Wilbur grumbled, who'd followed the rescue operation and now handed Chase some soap and a towel. "First those kids breaking into my bedroom, then some woman claims she got lost looking for the toilet, and now your cats."

"That woman was looking for something," I told Odelia. "And I have the impression it's got something to do with that film."

"Yeah, she's going to try and find Tex next," said Dooley.

This caused Odelia to frown.

"What did this woman look like?" she now asked Wilbur.

"I don't know and I don't care. Now can you please get lost? I can only leave my store unattended for so long, you know. I've got a business to run here, not a cat shelter."

And then he stomped out of the kitchen, always the busy storeowner.

"She was young and blond," I told our human.

"And she was very pretty," Dooley chimed in.

"Mh," said Odelia, then relayed our words to Chase, causing the latter to frown with concern.

"I think I know who this woman is," said the cop.

He took out his phone and started playing a movie. And as we all watched, I saw, for the very first time, the famous George Calhoun footage. And as the woman glanced up at Tex's overflying drone, I immediately recognized her, and so did Dooley.

"That's her!" I said.

"What are those people doing, Max?" asked Dooley now.

"Um, well they're kissing, Dooley," I said.

"Oh," he said, then asked, "But why aren't they wearing any clothes?"

"Because... they've been swimming, and sometimes people like to swim without any clothes on. It's more enjoyable that way."

His face cleared. "Of course! Because clothes cause friction, and without clothes you can swim a lot faster!" He then started to explain the details of his theory to Odelia, but our human wasn't listening. Instead she was clearly thinking hard, and it was obvious that this George Calhoun business was cause for great concern.

So I decided that maybe now wasn't a good time to broach the topic of the Pet Funnel 5000. Which was a pity, because I could have showed her the revolutionary pet flap in question, and Kingman could have demonstrated it to her and Chase.

Then again, if you want something, you have to pick your moments, and now didn't seem like the right time. It's all about delayed gratification, people.

And so as Odelia and Chase stood conferring, and I stood staring at the wonderful Pet Funnel 5000, suddenly my collar started beeping, and so did Dooley's. In fact they were beeping so loud, with lights flashing intermittently, that I had the distinct impression our fancy new collars had suddenly turned into a pair of explosive collars, and were about to go KABOOM!

13

As Odelia checked the app connected to her cats' collars, she saw that an alert had appeared in the form of a little red dot, and when she clicked the dot, it said that the collar was now in tracker mode, whatever that meant. She simply turned off the tracker mode, and the beeping stopped, much to the relief of both Max and Dooley.

"I thought I was going to explode!" said Max.

"Me, too!" Dooley cried.

"I have no idea why that happened," she intimated, as Chase looked over.

"What's that?" asked the cop as he gestured to the brain-wave mode.

"I should probably read the instructions," said Odelia. She clicked on the icon in the shape of a wave, and immediately got a graphic interface that seemed to show what was happening inside Max's brain.

"I wonder if you can somehow make that thing interpret their thoughts," said Chase, intrigued. The app looked like one of those screensavers, with plenty of wavy lines.

"I seemed to remember Vena saying that the brainwave

functionality is still in its infancy," said Odelia. "So for now it's just a lot of cool graphics but isn't operational." She tucked away her phone and decided to focus on other, more important stuff. "We need to figure out what to do about that film," she said. "First off, how is it possible that everybody suddenly seems to know about it? I thought you agreed to keep it a secret?"

Chase gave her a guilty look. "I talked to Alec this morning, and he confessed that he mentioned the film to Dolores. She's a huge George Calhoun fan, and he happened to mention what he saw, and even though he swore her to secrecy, you know what Dolores is like. She probably told her entire circle of friends, and all of her colleagues, and as a consequence now the story is doing the rounds of Hampton Cove."

She shook her head. Dolores Peltz, the police precinct's dispatcher-slash-receptionist, was probably the biggest blabbermouth in town. Which explained why Wilbur knew about the film, and so did George Calhoun's lady friend.

"Look," she said, after giving the matter some thought. "I think maybe the best thing would be for us to hand that film over to George and be done with it."

"But what if he sends his lawyer after us? We did film him on private property, so he probably has grounds to launch a suit."

"I have a feeling that if we hand back the film, he won't come after us. All he wants is for that film to disappear. He can handle the rumor and the innuendo. What he can't handle is actual footage being leaked online. That would ruin him, and destroy his marriage."

"Maybe you're right," said Chase. "I'll have to discuss it with your dad and your uncle first, but if they agree, we'll hand over the footage to George and that'll be the end of it."

Somehow Odelia had the impression it wouldn't be as

simple as all that, but at least it was a good start.

Her phone chimed and when she glanced at the display she saw that her editor was trying to reach her. "Dan has been bugging me to write an article about the George Calhoun film," she said.

"But I thought Dan didn't want the Gazette to wade into tabloid territory?"

"He doesn't, so instead he wants me to write a tongue-in-cheek article, alluding to the film, but not actually coming right out and tackling the subject."

"So he wants you to write about it, without writing about it."

"Something like that." She shrugged. "I'm heading down to the office. I need to discuss this with him face to face." Frankly she didn't want to listen to Dan trying to convince her to write that article for the umpteenth time that morning. Honestly, if the man wanted to publish an article about George Calhoun's romantic escapades, he probably should write it himself, since she really didn't feel like tackling the tacky topic herself.

She glanced down at Max and Dooley, and after making sure they were fine, and their recent adventure hadn't caused any lasting physical or emotional damage, she took off. She had a ton of work, and had already lost a lot of time saving her cats from treetops.

And she'd just left the store, and was on her way back to the paper, when suddenly a limo glided up to the curb and the door opened and a voice called out her name. When she glanced over, she saw that none other than George Calhoun himself was in the limo.

He'd taken off his sunglasses and was beckoning her over.

"Mrs. Kingsley," he said suavely. "Will you allow me the pleasure of your company?"

And since it's hard to say no to a global superstar like

George, she slipped into the limo, and soon the driver put the vehicle into motion again, and she found herself alone with George, who was holding up a bottle of champagne and two glasses.

She stared at the man, and when he seemed to realize that his offer was a little inappropriate, he promptly returned the champagne to a small fridge, and said ruefully, "I'm sorry for hijacking you like this, Mrs. Kingsley, but it has come to my attention that you might be the only person who can help me out of a particularly nasty spot of trouble."

"The drone footage," she said, nodding. She studied her surroundings. She'd never ridden in a limo as spectacularly opulent as this one before: the interior was all cream-colored leather, and it was a lot more spacious than you'd think from the outside.

"So you're admitting that you have the film," said George with satisfaction.

"My dad shot it accidentally, and I understand that you want it."

"I do," he said, "and I think you can easily understand why."

"Yes, I can," she said. "I'm sure your wife wouldn't appreciate that film turning up in the public domain."

The actor winced. "Look, I made a mistake. I should never have engaged in... relations with my neighbor's wife, but what's done is done, and I can't turn back the clock. All I want is for you and your family to give me a second chance. To prove I'm not that guy."

"You don't have to convince me, Mr. Calhoun."

"George, please," said the actor, who looked even more handsome in person than in the pictures or on the big screen. He had an engaging smile, and a twinkle in his eye.

"Frankly what you do in the privacy of your own home is of no concern to me, or my dad. If you want to have 'relations' with your neighbor's wife or all of your neighbors' wives, that's your business."

"I'm glad to hear it," said George, nodding with satisfaction. "So when I sent my lawyer to your father's house this morning, why didn't he comply? Why did he decide to keep the film?"

"Because your lawyer ambushed us," said Odelia. "And you have to admit his approach was a little heavy-handed—with his NDA and his legal threats."

"Sam does have a tendency to go all-out," said George with a tight smile.

"Look, I want to give you back that film, now all I need to do is convince my dad."

"How do you rate your chances?" asked George eagerly.

"I'm sure he'll agree," said Odelia, which caused the actor to break into a wide grin.

"You don't know what a relief that is to hear," he said. "When do you think I can have it?"

"Why don't you send your lawyer over again tonight? By then I'll have spoken to my dad."

"I tell you what—I'll come over personally. How does that sound?"

"That sounds great," said Odelia, much surprised. "My mom and gran will be thrilled."

"Then that's what we'll do, Mrs. Kingsley."

"Just call me Odelia," she said with a smile.

And as he pressed her hand warmly, then pressed a kiss on it like a real gentleman, she thought about asking him for an exclusive interview, but then decided against it. First they needed to get this whole business with the drone footage resolved, and maybe then she would ask him to sit down with her for an exclusive one-on-one. At least if by then he'd still look at her the way he was looking now: like a puppy receiving a favorite treat!

When Dooley and I returned home, I kept looking around, expecting that gang of kids to suddenly pop out from behind a tree or car. It's not a lot of fun knowing that you're being hunted, especially since cats are usually the hunters, not the hunted!

"I wonder if those kids will leave us in peace," I said as I nervously looked over to where a man was putting out the trash.

"I think so," said Dooley. "After Wilbur kicked them out they won't dare to come after us again."

"I wouldn't be so sure. One of them had to be saved by the fire department, and still they didn't think twice to break into Wilbur's house and try to grab us again."

"But what do they want with us, Max?"

"I have absolutely no idea, Dooley."

"Maybe they just like cats a lot?"

"If that's the case, they like us a little too much for my taste."

"Or maybe they've read Odelia's stories and now they want to meet us?"

It is true that Odelia writes plenty of stories featuring her cats, since people seem to like reading about our adventures, so maybe Dooley was onto something.

"So you think this could be a gang of fanatic fans?" I asked.

"Could be, Max. Fans do get a little fanatical from time to time. Like George Calhoun's fans, or Chuck Crush's. I've heard they go so far as to try and steal their underwear or their socks, just so they can feel closer to their idols."

"I hope they won't steal my underwear," I said as I glanced over to my right.

Dooley laughed. "Oh, Max, you're funny. You don't have any underwear!"

"And a good thing, too. Imagine what we would look like, wearing Calvins over our furs? Pretty silly if you ask me."

We'd finally arrived home in one piece, without encountering that vicious gang of kids again, and quickly made our way along the small strip of green that divides Odelia's house from her parents' place, and made our way through to the backyard... where we encountered Brutus and Harriet, looking distinctly rattled.

"What's going on?" I asked immediately,

"Oh, Max, we just went through the most horrible experience!" Harriet lamented.

"We were hunted," Brutus announced.

"Hunted? What do you mean?"

"A gang of young thugs showed up out of nowhere and followed us around everywhere," said Harriet. "They chased us up and down the street, and even up a tree!"

"Luckily we managed to get down by jumping to a nearby shed," said Brutus.

"But they were waiting for us, and we had to go on the run again!"

"Finally we managed to hide in a field full of brambles and nettles."

"And that seemed to do the trick. They stopped following us," Brutus concluded.

And I could see the evidence of his words in the pieces of bramble still sticking to his fur, and the nettles adorning Harriet's head.

"The same thing happened to us," said Dooley. "We had to be saved from a tree."

"Saved from a tree!" Harriet said, aghast.

"Chase had to get me out of a tree not once but twice," I said, not proud of my predicament.

"Kids?" asked Harriet, a hunted look in her green eyes.

"Kids," I confirmed somberly.

"I hate kids," Brutus growled.

"Me, too," I said.

"Oh, I like kids," said Dooley. "Except when they're chasing us around, of course."

"I don't know why they do this to us," Harriet lamented as she discovered a piece of nettle dangling from her ear and removed it with a look of extreme disgust.

"It must have something to do with our collars," said Brutus.

I blinked as his words registered. "You know, Brutus, you just might be right."

"Of course he's right," said Harriet. "Brutus is never wrong. Though you have to explain it to me again, honey bunny, cause I still don't understand how it works."

"I don't know how it works either, honey buns, but it can't be a coincidence that these kids started chasing us around the moment Vena gave us these collars." He gave me a somber look. "They called me MokeBrutus. Can you imagine?"

"They called me MokeMax," I said.

"I think I heard them call me MokeHarriet," said Harriet.

"And I'm MokeDooley," said Dooley cheerfully.

"It must have something to do with this Mokemon business," I said. "It's owned by the same company that makes our collars. Though what the collars have to do with these kids is frankly beyond me."

"They did seem to know exactly where we were, didn't they, Max?" said Dooley. "So maybe our collars are somehow connected to their phones?"

"Do you think they hacked our collars, Max?" asked Harriet. "Is that even possible?"

"Vena said they were hacker proof," said Brutus.

"Vena said a lot of things," I said. "I just hope it's over and done with now. Those kids took years off my life."

"And a lot of flab, too," said Brutus, patting my belly. "So when are we starting our training regimen, buddy?"

"Um…" I said, not exactly looking forward to Brutus becoming my personal trainer. Somehow I imagined blood, sweat and tears would become part of my future if he became my fitness coach.

"Oh, Max has the most amazing idea about our pet flap, you guys," said Dooley, and proceeded to apprise our friends of the marvelous new Pet Funnel 5000. And as he brought them up to speed, I suddenly thought I saw a head appearing in the rose bushes lining the back of the garden. And as I watched closer, my heart immediately sped up, for I was sure it was those pesky kids again. But then I saw that it wasn't kids but a grown man!

"Guys!" I hissed. "There's a man hiding in the bushes!"

"I know," said Harriet. "It's Chuck Crush."

"Chuck Crush!"

"Yeah, imagine that: Chuck Crush hiding in our bushes!"

"I think he's waiting for Odelia," said Brutus. "He's been there ever since we got home."

"He thinks we can't see him," Harriet said with a giggle. "But of course we noticed immediately."

"He's naked," I said when the man popped up again, before disappearing from view.

"Yeah, he's wearing boxers," said Harriet.

"But why?" I said, much bewildered.

Harriet shrugged. "Your guess is as good as mine, Max."

"There are tribes in the Amazon Rainforest who never wear clothes," Dooley said. "So maybe Chuck Crush is a member of one of those tribes?"

And as we watched, Chuck popped up again, before slowly sinking out of view, like a submerging vessel.

And then suddenly I noticed how a second head appeared, a few bushes to Chuck's right. It was the same blond woman we'd seen over at the General Store, searching Wilbur's bedroom. She, too, was bobbing in and out of view, presumably unaware that Chuck was close by, but luckily in her case she was fully dressed.

"Look, there's another one," I said, gesturing to the blond woman.

"I don't know what this world is coming to," Harriet lamented. "Kids chasing us up trees, naked men and women hiding in the bushes. Strange things are happening, you guys, and I'm not sure I can explain what it's all about."

Just then, Odelia arrived home, and immediately Chuck emerged and walked up to her. He was indeed naked, apart from a pair of boxers with a unicorn motif, and had plastered his most charming smile on his face. But when he saw Chase following behind Odelia, that smile quickly disappeared, and the famous actor performed an abrupt about-face, and headed back to his trusty bushes, where, like Tarzan, he presumably felt more at ease, reminding him as they did of his homeland in the Amazon Rainforest, and the naked tribe to which he no doubt belonged.

Odelia and Chase, who'd witnessed the scene in wordless surprise, now stared at one another, and would probably have commented on the peculiar scene if not suddenly the blond woman walked up to them, also smiling her most charming smile.

"Hi, there," she said. "I'm Tammy." And to show them that she came in peace, she held out a hand, which Odelia lightly shook, and so did Chase. "Now you're probably wondering what I'm doing here, but you folks have got something that belongs to me, and I would like to have it back." She gave Chase a wink. "You know what I mean."

"Um…" said Chase, who looked much impressed by this very attractive woman.

Suddenly Chuck piped up from behind the bushes, "Excuse me, but that film belongs to me."

"No, it doesn't, Chuck," said the woman. "So butt out." Apparently Tammy had spotted Chuck, which didn't surprise me, for his attempts at obfuscation were ham-fisted at best.

Chuck now popped up from his bush again, and approached, diffident at first, like a timid butterfly, then asserting himself with more vigor. "Look, that film features my best bud, and I think it's only fair that you hand it to me, his official emissary in this delicate matter."

"That film also features me, Chuck," said Tammy. "So it clearly belongs to me."

"George told me that he wants that film, and what George wants, George gets."

Both the actor and the blonde now turned to Odelia and Chase, who'd been eying the scene with astonishment written all over their faces, and it was a testament to the strangeness of the scene that the first words out of Odelia's mouth were, "Why aren't you dressed, Chuck?"

"Does it bother you?"

"No, it's fine," said Odelia, as she took in the man's bronzed and athletic features.

"It's because it reminds him of his tribe," said Dooley knowingly.

"Look, that film is mine, and I want it," said Tammy.

"You're in it," said Chase, finally finding his voice. It wasn't a question so much as a statement of fact.

"That's what I said. Oh, you've seen it!" She smiled. "So you know I'm not lying." She held out her hand, her fingernails painted a pretty pink. "Just give it to Tammy, there's a good boy."

"Oh, but I don't have it," said Chase. "Or at least not the original."

"Look, neither of you should bother," said Odelia now, having sufficiently recovered from her surprise for her brain to have rebooted and work at regular capacity once more. "I promised George I'd hand him back that film tonight, so you can both go home and rest easy. No one will get to see that film except George."

The woman's face took on a mulish expression. "But I don't *want* George to get the film. I'm in it, too, so I have just as much right as him to get my hands on it."

"No, you don't," said Chuck. "All you want is to publish that film and reap the rewards of sudden infamy. And I for one am not gonna let you." He held out his hand. "So please give it to me before this gold digger ruins George's life."

"Who are you calling a gold digger, you sad excuse for a human being?" said Tammy, getting a little hot under her collar now.

"There's no need to get worked up," said Chase, the peacemaker in him manifesting itself. "We'll arrange things directly with George tonight, and that'll be the end of it."

Tammy seemed to know when she was beaten, for she now started to walk away. "Don't think you can get away with this," she said, wagging a reproachful finger in our direction. "If George thinks he can screw me over, he's got another thing coming."

We all watched as Tammy disappeared around the corner, and frankly I was relieved. She was clearly a very forceful personality, and I didn't think I liked her very much. Chuck also seemed to relax, for his sixpack now turned into a four-pack, then into a twopack, then was gone, a clear sign he was easing up on those all-important abdominal muscles.

"You weren't kidding when you said you were going to hand that film to George?" he asked uncertainly.

"No, I wasn't," said Odelia with a smile. "I saw George earlier, and I promised him I'd talk to my dad and I did. And he thinks it's a good idea to hand the film back to George."

"And hopefully it will put this matter to bed once and for all," said Chase.

Chuck grinned at this. "Put this matter to bed. Cop humor. I love it." But Chase wasn't kidding, and it showed from the stern expression on his face, causing Chuck's grin to quickly dissipate. "Look, I'm sorry," he said. "But when George asked me to do everything in my power to get that film back for him, I told him I would, and I have. He's my best friend. I'd do anything for that man."

"Even enter my mom's bathroom dressed like that?" asked Odelia.

"I'm always dressed like this," said Chuck with a shrug. "I hate the feeling of clothes against my skin."

"Oh, I think I've heard of that," said Dooley. "It's a medical condition. Some people can't stand the sensation of clothes next to their skin, so they like to walk around in the nude all the time."

"I think Chuck is just walking around like that to make an impression on Marge and Odelia, Dooley," I said. "Hoping to convince them to hand over the film."

"Make an impression? I don't understand, Max," said Dooley.

"Let's just say that some women are more susceptible to a man's arguments when he's not wearing any clothes."

Dooley stared at Chuck, then back to me, and it was obvious he still didn't get it, but at that moment, Chuck must have figured that he'd finally outstayed his welcome, and said his goodbyes before absconding from the scene.

"Looks like soon we'll finally have our peace and quiet back," said Chase. "And not a minute too soon."

"Dad said he'll be happy when he's finally rid of that film," said Odelia.

And as our humans walked into the house to discuss the terms of the handover, I glanced back at our pet flap, and wondered if this was the right time to discuss the Pet Funnel 5000. I decided it wasn't. Better wait until after this drone business was finally over and done with. Odelia would be happy, and more susceptible to my arguments.

15

*D*ooley was staring before him and thinking hard. He still didn't fully comprehend why that film was so important to George. So the man had kissed a woman who wasn't his wife, that much he understood, but why was everybody so eager to get their hands on that film? Wasn't it nice of George to be kissing a woman? It was, after all, what he did in his movies, so why did he think his wife would be upset if she discovered the truth?

It was a mystery to him, and he thought about asking Max, but his friend seemed so involved with his pet flap issue Dooley didn't think it was a good idea to bother him with this particular question.

No, he felt he should probably be able to work it out by himself. And so when the doorbell chimed and Marge went to open the door and a woman walked into the living room who looked very much like George Calhoun's wife, Dooley thought that maybe now he would get his answer. Who better than George's wife to explain why she was so upset about her husband's infidelities?

"Take a seat, Mrs. Calhoun," said Marge, who seemed

impressed at the sudden insertion into her home of this woman. Anna Calhoun was a very attractive woman, in a classical sense. She wasn't blond, like George's girlfriend, who appeared to be his neighbor's wife, but dark-haired and more sophisticated in her appearance. She had sharp and fine-boned features, and was dressed in fine and, so Dooley thought, very expensive clothes. She was also holding a small black leather Louis Vuitton clutch.

"What can I do for you?" asked Marge.

"I think you know why I'm here, Mrs. Poole," said the woman now.

"Um… I'm not sure…"

"You don't have to spare my feelings," said Anna Calhoun, proudly tilting her chin. "It has come to my attention that a film exists, showing my husband in close embrace with Tammy Freiheit, who is our neighbor. Is it true?"

Marge seemed reluctant to divulge the truth, maybe to spare the woman's feelings, but finally cast down her eyes and nodded. "It is true," she said quietly.

"I knew it," said Anna, as she glanced to the television, where one of George's old movies was playing. And as luck would have it, he was just in that moment kissing a woman passionately and with plenty of obvious fervor.

"Can I see the film?" asked Anna, dragging her eyes away from the passionate scene.

Marge nodded, and called out, "Tex? Come in here a moment, will you?"

Tex came running, his mouth working as he'd just shoved a piece of cheese into it, and wiping his hands on a towel. When he caught sight of their distinguished guest, he abruptly swallowed the cheese and dropped the towel.

"This is Anna," said Marge. "She would like to watch the footage you shot with that drone of yours."

"Um…" said Tex, glancing to his wife. "Are you sure that's a good idea?" he whispered.

"I can hear you, Mr. Poole," said Anna, "and I can assure you it's a very good idea. Now please find it in your heart to put me out of my misery and show me the footage of my husband with this other woman."

Tex blinked rapidly, but then nodded and removed himself from the room. Dooley heard him stomp up the stairs, then stomp back down again, carrying a laptop and a USB stick. He proceeded to open the laptop and insert the USB stick into the computer, then place it on the living room table. Moments later, the same film started to play that Dooley had seen a part of before, on Chase's phone.

Anna sat there, unmoving, her face not displaying a single trace of emotion, as she watched her husband kissing a woman who clearly wasn't her. Finally, as George looked up at the sky, and threw a rock at the drone, the film ended and Anna seemed to wipe away a small tear.

"Thank you so much," she said finally. "Can you please give me a copy? I need it for my divorce lawyer."

And she took a small USB stick from her purse and handed it to Tex, who proceeded to put a copy of the incriminating evidence on the stick, and hand it back to her. She safely tucked it away into her purse, closed it with a snap, then rose to her feet, graciously thanked all those present, and walked out, proud until the last moment.

Marge and Tex just stood there for a few moments after Anna had left, then Marge said, "Wow. What a woman."

"I don't think George will like this," said Tex.

"What did he expect? You can't fool around with your neighbor's wife and expect there won't be consequences."

"So why is Anna so upset?" asked Dooley now. But Marge seemed deaf to his question, and as she disappeared into the kitchen, and Tex closed his laptop, Dooley still had no idea why everyone was behaving as if they were at a funeral.

Lucky for him Gran walked in, eager to watch Jeopardy, and when Dooley had apprised her of the facts as they'd transpired, Gran said, "Now look, Dooley, when a woman marries a man, she expects that man to be faithful to her, see? And when that man starts cavorting with other women, it's very painful for her to know, and even more painful to watch, see?"

"But George is an actor, Gran," said Dooley. "He kisses other women all the time. So why is this time different?"

"Because this time, Dooley, he was kissing that woman for real, not just for the movie."

"But... doesn't he kiss those other women in the movie for real, too?"

Gran thought about this for a moment. "I guess you've got a point. Though he can always tell his wife the director made him do it."

"So what's going to happen now?" asked Dooley.

"What's going to happen is that George will probably have a lot explaining to do."

16

That night, we all waited for George to arrive and take possession of his latest hit movie, as captured by drone, but when the clock had finally struck eleven, we had to accept that he wasn't going to show up, and it probably had something to do with his wife's visit. First Tex and Marge decided to retire, followed by Gran, and finally Odelia and Chase returned to their home, and so did Dooley and myself, with Harriet and Brutus staying behind to keep their humans company as they chewed on the remarkable decision by Mr. Calhoun not to pick up his film.

"His wife is probably giving him hell right now," said Chase as we traversed the backyard and moved into our home.

"I don't blame her," said Odelia. "If I caught you with our neighbor I wouldn't like it either."

"You mean if you caught me on film with Kurt you would be upset?" Chase quipped.

Kurt Mayfield is our next-door neighbor, a retired music teacher and the proud owner of a Yorkshire Terrier, who's also a dear friend, unlikely as that may sound for a cat to consider a dog one of his best friends. But then that's cats for you: we like to keep you on your toes!

"Let's go to bed," said Odelia as she checked if she'd turned off the stove. "I'll call George in the morning."

And so our humans retired for the night, and Dooley and I, after eating our fill, and taking the opportunity to make good use of our respective litter boxes, decided that now that the humans had all gone to bed, the night, which was still young, was ours, and it was time to head down to cat choir and enjoy the pleasant company of our friends.

Once again, Odelia had been so kind to leave the door ajar, so I could slip in and out without any problems.

As we moved into the backyard next door, to await Harriet and Brutus's arrival so we could head out together, suddenly I became aware of a dark-clad figure placing a ladder against the wall and moving up said ladder, while a second black-clad figure was holding that ladder and making sure his or her friend wouldn't topple over and break their neck.

"Look, Max," said Dooley. "Two burglars are breaking into the house."

He said it as if it was the most natural thing in the world. And as I watched, slack-jawed, as the twosome pushed Gran's bedroom window open, moments later a loud cry ripped the silence of the night to shreds, and the burglar came clambering back down the same ladder and the twosome quickly skedaddled. But not before a very irate-looking Gran appeared in the upstairs window, shaking her fist and screaming, "I saw your face, Jerry Vale. And if I ever catch you it won't be your lucky day!"

"I'm sorry, Mrs. Muffin," a loud voice cried out in the night, and I recognized the voice as belonging to Johnny Carew, one of Gran's friends, who unfortunately has a slightly criminal bent.

Gran shook her head in dismay, then retracted her head, and moments later, all was quiet once more.

But not for long, for that same ladder, which still stood against the wall, was now being used by a second burglar, who also moved up the thing, pushed open Gran's window to crawl in, and moments later came crawling back out, looking a little the worse for wear, with Gran appearing with a hockey stick clutched in her hands, as she wielded it with practiced ease. The man was now making the short trip from the second floor to ground level in record time, as he didn't even use the ladder but simply dropped down, landing on the lawn with a dull thud. He seemed dazed for a moment, as he just sat there, catching his breath, with Gran screaming, "You messed with the wrong woman!"

And as the man's mask had slipped, I now saw how the same paparazzo who'd accosted us earlier that day was hiding underneath. He scrambled to his feet, and took off, hitting the road, same way Johnny and Jerry had done.

"Looks like a busy night for burglars, Max," Dooley commented.

"Yeah, looks like," I agreed.

"What do you think they want?"

"Why, that film, of course. What else?"

"But why? What's so important about that film that everybody wants it?"

"That paparazzo probably can sell that film for a lot of money," I said. "And the same goes for those two crooks."

"Look, Max. There's another one," said Dooley, interrupting my train of thought.

He was right: before our very eyes, suddenly another dark-clad person crawled up that ladder, and made his way into Gran's room. The old lady must have been waiting for him, though, for her reaction time was getting shorter and shorter by the burglar. This time it only took her a couple of seconds to hit the guy over the head with her hockey stick, and as we watched, he performed the same ungracious landing on the backyard turf. His mask slipped, and a man we'd never seen before appeared. And as Gran found it expedient to hit him with what looked like a hockey puck, the man quickly picked himself up from the ground and took off, choosing the same route the others had taken—a sound choice, as Gran was now beyond herself with anger. "And stay out!" she screamed.

Her cries of distress had attracted the attention of the others, for the light came on in Tex and Marge's bedroom, who both stuck their heads out the window to see what was going on. Next door, the Trappers also appeared, Marcie and Ted, and soon Odelia and Chase also joined the minor mob scene. And while the humans discussed this unexpected crime wave, all standing on the lawn, they were joined by Kurt Mayfield, who said that he thought having a cop for a neighbor would have cut down on crime, but it now looked as if it had only made things worse instead.

Brutus and Harriet were finally ready to go out, and so we decided to let the humans deal with the burglarious elements and enjoy a nice and relaxing time at cat choir instead.

And as we hit the street, we first came upon Johnny and Jerry sitting in their car and discussing recent events.

"Looks like we won't be able to get our mitts on that film, Jer," said Johnny, the biggest of the two crooks.

"No thanks to you," said Jerry, as he removed his mask. "If you hadn't pointed me to the wrong bedroom we would have gotten away with this."

"I know you said we could sell that film for a million bucks, Jer, but what you forgot to mention is that it was the Pooles we needed to burgle."

"It doesn't matter who we need to burgle, Johnny. Whoever's got that film is who we need to burgle."

"But I like the Pooles, Jer."

"Well, I don't. Every time we get involved with these people, something goes wrong, and we end up doing time."

And then Jerry put the car in gear and they took off.

The next car contained the paparazzo, who was on the phone. "No, Frank, I couldn't get my hands on that film. It's being guarded. Yeah, I know you said you'd offer me a hundred grand, but if I can't get it, I can't get it. I mean, have you tried to steal something from under the nose of a cop? Huh? No? Well, I have, and it's not a lot of fun!"

The next car contained the dark horse in this race. He was also on the phone. "No, Tammy, I couldn't get it. Some old broad attacked me with a hockey stick. I almost broke my neck. So next time you've got a great idea, you better do it yourself!" And with these words of love and devotion, he hung up the phone, then took off, tires screaming, and making a lot of noise for a man driving a car in a residential area so late at night.

"I think it's safe to say that was Tammy's husband," said Harriet.

"The woman George was… kissing," I said, eyeing Dooley closely.

But he gave me a reassuring smile. "Gran explained it all to me, Max. There's a big difference when George kisses a woman because the director tells him to, and when he kisses her without a director. In the first case he can tell his wife he won't get paid if he doesn't do what the director says, and in the second case he has no excuse."

"Well done, Dooley," said Harriet, and patted our friend on the back. "Looks like you're finally up to date with this whole strange episode."

"I like to think so," said Dooley proudly. "Now all we need to do is find out why George didn't show up."

"Because his wife found out," said Brutus. "So now it doesn't matter anymore."

Brutus was probably right. And as we went on our way, I decided I wasn't going to let my mind wander to George and his marital issues but enjoy cat choir instead. After all, humans always have something going on, but so do cats, and why should I spend all of my valuable time worrying about their business, when I have my own stuff to deal with? Such as there are: the group of kids waiting around the corner, and uttering loud cries when they saw us!

17

I don't know if you've ever been attacked by a pack of wild kids, but I can assure you it's not a lot of fun!

For one thing, kids are fast—they can run like the wind! Luckily cats are pretty fast, too. Except for me, on account of my bone situation. And so the kids would have caught up with me, if not suddenly a car had stopped at the curb, a hand had stolen out, grabbed me by the scruff of the neck, and dragged me into the vehicle.

The door closed behind me, and as I was dumped on the backseat, the car took off with screaming tires, causing those kids to stare after us, having nothing to show for their frantic pursuit. I could hear them shout in the distance, and it sounded a lot like, "MokeMax! Come back, MokeMax!"

Whoever or whatever MokeMax was, I was glad for the reprieve. Or at least I should have been, but when I glanced over to the driver, I saw that I was in the presence of none other than Johnny and Jerry. Now I wasn't exactly sure if I should be relieved or alarmed, but for the moment at least I was safe from that baying pack of wild kids, so that was one thing to be grateful for.

"Okay, we're back in business," said Jerry, who was behind the wheel.

"I'm glad we saved him, Jer," said Johnny as he turned in his seat and tickled me under the chin. "Those kids looked mean. Didn't those kids look mean, Max? Yeah, they did. Oh, yeah, they did. Chasing you around like that."

I purred a little, for that was what the big lug seemed to expect.

"And I'm glad we got some leverage," said Jerry.

"What do you mean, leverage?" asked Johnny.

"You know—for the film."

"You're not thinking of abducting Max, are you, Jer?"

"We're not abducting him. We're just keeping him as leverage, in exchange for that film." He glanced over to his partner. "Oh, don't look at me like that, Johnny. It's business —plain and simple."

"We can't do that," said the big guy. "He's Marge's cat, and you know how much Marge cares for the orange fatty."

Immediately I stopped purring. I vehemently dislike being called orange, on account of the fact that I'm blorange, not orange.

"Look, it's very simple. We tell Marge to hand over the film, in exchange for her cat. Easy peasy, no harm done."

"I don't think we should do that, Jer," said Johnny.

"Who cares what you think? I'm the brains in this outfit, and you're the brawn, or have you forgotten who gets you out of trouble each and every time?"

"And I say you can't do that, Jer," said Johnny, and for once in his life the big guy was actually displaying some backbone.

"Says who?" Jerry sneered.

"Says me," said Johnny decidedly.

And to show his partner what he meant, he pressed his big foot down on the brakes, presumably pulverizing his partner's much smaller digit, causing the latter to scream, "Hey, what do you think you're doing, you dumbbell!"

"I'm doing what's right," said Johnny. And as the car careened across the road and finally screeched to a halt, he opened the door, and said, "Out, Max. Now."

And as I gave him a grateful look, I did as he suggested.

"You idiot!" said Jerry.

"We're not evil, Jer."

"He's getting away!"

"Good. He should get away. Run, little fellow, run home to Marge," he urged me on.

And so I did run. Not home to Marge, cause I just came from there, but away from the wannabe kidnappers. And I probably would have reached the park in one piece, if I hadn't once again come upon that gang of kids. This time they looked a little dejected, after having failed to capture me. But the moment they caught sight of me, they immediately perked up. And just for the smiles on those faces I would have let them capture me—not!

Once again, I was forced to shift into high gear, and moments later was running at full tilt, crossing backyards and making my way in the dark, those kids hot on my trail. I don't know how they did it, but they seemed to know exactly where I was going at all times. When I swerved left, they swerved left. When I ducked right, they ducked right, too! And then it finally dawned on me: Brutus was right. They were tracking my collar. There was no other explanation! And so I finally ripped the thing from my neck and left it where it dropped, and hid underneath a rhododendron tree to see what happened next. And sure enough: the kids all gathered around the collar, their phones held out in front of them.

"Where did he go?" asked the freckled kid.

"I don't know," said the blond girl. "He just disappeared."

She picked up the collar, eyed it curiously, then pocketed it as if it were the spoils of war, and moved on.

I breathed a deep sigh of relief as I watched them walk away. Odelia might have been able to track my health with the collar, but it was now obvious that the collar was in fact a danger to that health, and my wellbeing!

18

*O*delia watched as her uncle took Gran's statement in regards to the multiple attempts to break into her home, when suddenly her phone produced a loud beeping sound. She picked it out of her pocket and stared at the app in question with concern. It was the Better Pet Yet app, and the notification told her that Max's heartbeat and brainwaves had unexpectedly been terminated. And when she opened the app, it said, 'Terminal error!'

Her heart rate spiked when she realized that according to the app… Max had just been killed!

Immediately she glanced around, and when she couldn't find her cats, asked her mom and then her grandma, but they hadn't seen them either.

"I saw them earlier," Chase indicated, "but they seem to have disappeared."

She held the app in front of her husband's nose. "According to this thing Max is dead, Chase. He's dead!"

Chase took the phone and studied the app intently. "It doesn't say that he's dead. It just says it lost connection to the chip monitoring his vital signs."

"Which means he's dead!"

"Which means he's not wearing his collar right now. He could have taken it off. Or it could have malfunctioned."

Only slightly mollified by this sample of excellent reasoning, she glanced down at the app, and saw that her three other cats were still in the vicinity, as evidenced by the three little dots moving on a map of Hampton Cove, but Max was not among them.

A wave of panic washed over her, and she leaned on her husband for support. "You gotta help me, Chase. If I lost Max, I don't know what I'd do."

"Easy, babe. I'm sure he's fine. You know Max. He knows how to take care of himself. He's a clever puss, and has managed to get out of plenty of tough spots before."

"But he's not on the map, Chase!" she practically screamed.

He took the phone, messed with the app's controls, and finally said, "I think I've got him—or at least I've got his signal." And he pointed to a little red dot that was, indeed, moving. It also said that it was this dot that wasn't registering any signs of life at that moment. "Let's just follow the dot," Chase suggested, "and see what we find, all right?"

She nodded, and chewed her lower lip in distinct concern over the fate of Max.

And as they left Uncle Alec and one of his officers to do the honors and interview all the neighbors who'd flocked to the backyard in connection with this sudden spate of burglaries, she and Chase followed the little red dot. And soon they were walking along, with Odelia fervently hoping that Max was all right, and hadn't been harmed in any way.

"We had him," said Ralphie dejectedly. "We had him and he slipped through our fingers."

"We'll get him next time," said his sister Lisa.

"No, we won't. This time he gave us the slip for real," said Mike, who'd been the first in their small band of friends to get hooked on the new Mokemon game.

"The others are still out there," said Jake, the Benjamin of the gang. "We should go after them next."

"They won't net us as many points as MokeMax," Ralphie pointed out.

"I just don't understand what happened," said Jackson, who was the tallest of the group, and stuck out not just because of his height, but also because of his red curly hair. "How can a Mokemon simply disappear like that?"

"Maybe it's a glitch?" Lisa suggested.

"I don't think so," said Ralphie as he studied the collar he still held in his hand. They were in their local park, where they liked to meet, and where they'd discovered that the Mokemons they liked to hunt spent most of their time, especially at night.

"I don't understand what this is," said Lisa. "Mokemons are fictitious, right? So how come MokeMax was wearing a collar?"

"I think I know what's going on here," said Jackson, who wasn't just the tallest and hairiest, but also the smartest of the outfit. "This is the latest iteration of the game. And it's based on old technology that somehow they've managed to turn into something way cool." He looked at the others with delight. "Holograms, people!"

"Holograms?" said Mike, giving their friend a skeptical look.

"Holograms! Just think about it: how come we can see these new Mokemons? Because they're actually there, only they're not really there, of course. They're being produced with these collars. It's a high-tech instrument designed to produce a holographic effect in the real world. I bet it can fly, too, which is why the Mokemons can move so fast. Only this one must have malfunctioned, which is why MokeMax suddenly disappeared, and we were left holding his collar."

"So… MokeMax is actually inside this collar somehow?" said Lisa, staring at the thing.

"Yes, he is," said Jackson, clearly proud to have figured out what had baffled the others.

"So… how do we fix it?" asked Ralphie, who really wanted to bring MokeMax back to life so they could catch him.

"I'm not sure," said Jackson as he subjected the collar to closer scrutiny. "Look," he said, and they all looked.

"It's the logo of the Mokemon company!" said Lisa.

More cries of excitement filled the air. "You were right, Jackson," said Ralphie. "This collar… *is* MokeMax!"

And as Jackson placed the collar onto a flat rock, they all bowed their heads in deference to the greatest Mokemon to have hit the world in recent years: MokeMax.

"MokeMax, please come back to us," said Lisa. "We miss you."

"Yeah, we miss you, MokeMax," Ralphie chimed in.

"What the hell is going on here!" suddenly a harsh voice intruded upon their reverent meditation on the greatness of the great MokeMax.

"And what have you done with my cat!" a female voice added itself to the interruption of this sacred moment.

The five kids looked up as one kid, and saw they were being approached by a man and a woman, who both looked very angry indeed. The man was built like a lumberjack, and the woman, petite and fair-haired, appeared to be so angry she was on the verge of breathing fire through her nostrils. Her name might as well have been Daenerys.

"We-we were talking about MokeMax," said Ralphie, surprised by this sudden emergence onto the scene of these two adults. He knew adults rarely understood how wonderful and exciting the world of Mokemon was, but he now sensed there was more to it than that. Maybe they didn't approve of five kids being out in the park at night?

"What have you done with Max?!" the woman demanded. She grabbed the collar and held it up. "Did you kill him?"

"Oh, no, of course not," said Lisa, shocked by the accusation.

"We tried to catch him, but he got away," said Ralphie.

"We think the collar malfunctioned and MokeMax's hologram disappeared," Jackson explained his theory.

"What are you talking about?" said the woman. "Where is Max?"

"Well… I guess you could say he's inside the collar?" said Jackson, speaking extra-slowly now, since obviously these two didn't have the first clue about Mokemon.

The woman stared at the collar and then at Jackson. "You mean that Max disappeared… into his collar?"

Jackson nodded furiously. "That's exactly what happened. But if you go online you'll probably find a FAQ on how to fix the collar, and maybe bring MokeMax back to life."

"What's all this nonsense about Moké Mons?" asked the guy with the many muscles as he took the collar from the woman and eyed it suspiciously.

"MokeMax is one of four new Mokemons that were launched this week," Ralphie explained. "Mokemon, which stands for Mock Monsters, is a brand owned and operated by Intended2," he added when the two grownups just stared at him as if he'd suddenly grown a third ear or a second nose or something. It was tedious having to explain basic stuff like this to adults, but he was used to it by now, having had to explain the brilliance of Mokemon to three aunts, two uncles, four grandparents and his mom and dad.

"MokeMax is the coolest of the four," said Lisa.

"And he nets you the most points if you capture him."

"Though MokeDooley is also pretty cute."

"I like MokeBrutus best," said Mike.

"I like MokeHarriet," said Jake devotedly. "She's so cute."

"MokeDooley is actually the least interesting new Mokemon," said Ralphie.

"You're only saying that because he only nets you half the points," said his sister.

"MokeDooley?" said the woman, shaking her head as if trying to wake up from some nightmarish dream.

"Okay, so they're all pretty cool," said Ralphie, "but MokeMax is the best. He's brave, he's handsome, he's big, but most importantly, he's blorange. Not orange, mind you—blorange. And yes, there's a big difference."

"MokeMax is also very versatile," said Jackson, not stinting on the MokeMax praise, as they all had become big fans in the short time since MokeMax had become part of the big Mokemon family.

"Yeah, you should have seen him this morning, climbing that tree as if he'd never done anything else his entire life," said Lisa with a laugh.

"Or when he escaped from the General Store," said Jake. "That was way cool!"

"Okay, enough," said the woman, who'd been following the back-and-forth with rapt attention. "Where did you say Max... MokeMax's collar broke down?"

"Um... must have been on the corner of Harrington Street?" said Mike.

"Yeah, Harrington Street," Ralphie agreed. "He'd just been dumped from a car, and that's when we spotted him."

"It's been tough tracking him," said Lisa, "since the app keeps breaking down."

"I don't think it's the app breaking down but the hologram," Jackson said. "I think the technology isn't fully developed yet. It might even still be in beta."

The woman now smiled for the first time since they'd made her acquaintance, though she still hadn't formally introduced herself. She now held out her hand and said, "My name is Odelia Kingsley, and this is my husband Chase Kingsley. We're the proud owners of Max, who's a real cat, by the way, and not a hologram." She held up the collar. "I bought this collar for him on the advice of his vet, who said it would make it easier to track his health—heartrate, blood pressure, and so on."

Ralphie frowned at the woman. "What are you saying, lady?"

"I think she's saying that MokeMax isn't a Mokemon but an actual cat," said Mike.

"That's right. There is no MokeMax, though I'm sure that when I tell him about this, he'll find it very flattering, the way you just spoke about him."

"So this collar…" said Lisa.

"Is exactly that: a cat collar. Only the company who produces these collars is the same company who are behind this game you like so much. This Mock…"

"Mokemon," said Ralphie with a frown.

Jackson snapped his fingers. "They must have made a programming mistake," he said. "Somehow the software that runs these collars must have bled into the Mokemon universe."

"You mean… we've been hunting an actual cat all day?" asked Lisa, looking horrified.

"Not just any cat," said Mrs. Kingsley. "My cat. In fact all four of my cats: Max, Dooley, Harriet and Brutus."

"So… none of them is an actual Mokemon?" asked Mike.

"No, they're four actual cats, all wearing cat collars."

"Oh, crap," said Ralphie, and he voiced what the others were all thinking.

"I'm so sorry, Mrs. Kingsley," said Lisa. "We had no idea."

"When the four new Mokemons suddenly popped up on our phones, we were so excited, since they only appeared in Hampton Cove, and nowhere else around the country."

"So we figured we were the first who'd been given the opportunity to capture them," Lisa continued to explain.

"I think you better call off the hunt now," said Mr. Kingsley in a deep rumbling voice.

"Of course, sir," said Ralphie, then eyed the man a little closer. "Say, aren't you a cop?"

"Yes, I am," Mr. Kingsley confirmed, which caused the four other kids to gulp.

"Are-are we under arrest now, officer?" asked Mike.

The cop allowed his facial muscles to twitch into what could loosely be interpreted as a smile. "No, you're not under arrest, but I will advise you to quit hunting my wife's cats."

There was a threat implied in the man's words, though Ralphie couldn't exactly put his finger on it. Still, he quickly said, "Of course, sir. We'll call off the chase. Won't we, guys?"

"Y-yes, o-officer," said Mike with a distinct lack of bravado.

"Do you want us to help you find MokeMax—I mean Max, Mrs. Kingsley?" asked Lisa.

"Yes, I would appreciate that very much," said Mrs. Kingsley.

And so the five kids set out, accompanied by Mr. and Mrs. Kingsley, to hunt down MokeMax one last time—though this time they couldn't rely on the Mokemon app on their phones, only on their own sense of direction and their smarts.

Ralphie certainly hoped Max would be fine, for even though Officer Kingsley had said he wouldn't arrest them, he still had the distinct impression that if Max wasn't found before the morning, there would be hell to pay. And how was he going to explain *that* to his parents?

19

I have to admit I'd had enough excitement for one day, so after being abducted, kicked out of a car, and chased by those crazy kids, I felt enough was enough, and decided to go home and enjoy a nice nap for the rest of the night, and maybe until well into the next day, too!

Of course when I arrived home, my friends were nowhere to be found—probably singing their hearts out at cat choir—and of Chase and Odelia there was not a single trace either—presumably still trying to figure out who'd dared to burgle the house next door.

And so it was a distinct sense of gratification that first I ate my fill in kibble, then did my business in my litter box, making a nice donation after the excitement I'd gone through, then mounted the stairs at my leisure, jumped on the bed (and made it at the first attempt—take that, Vena!), curled up into a ball and went straight to sleep.

I like the company of humans, of course, and the company of my fellow felines, but sometimes a cat just wants to be alone, if you know what I mean.

And so while the world turned, I slept the sleep of the young and the restless. Or is the bold and the beautiful?

And I felt pretty refreshed when at long last Odelia and Chase decided to call it a night as well, and entered the bedroom. Their cries of dismay woke me up from a very nice dream of what paradise must be like: a place filled with kibble-laden golden plates as far as the eye can see. As I opened one eye, awakened by the ruckus, I found myself gazing into Odelia's face, and I must say she looked at me a little strangely. And then suddenly she heaved a startled cry and moments later hugged me so tight I had trouble breathing!

"Max!" she cried with a distinct quiver in her voice. "You're all right!"

"I know I'm all right," I said as I yawned cavernously. "That's the way I roll."

"But… you lost your collar!" she said, and showed me the proof of her statement by presenting me with the collar.

I gave the contraption a look of distaste. "Those kids tried to catch me again," I said, "until I realized this thing is what must have put them on my trail, so I decided to rip it off and lo and behold: problem solved!"

"Oh, Max!'" she said, and once more gave me one of those bone-crushing hugs you always read about. And then she promptly burst into a flood of tears!

"There, there," I said as I watched the strange scene unfold. I glanced up at Chase, who stood behind his woman, and even the big strong detective was suffering from a certain moistness about the eyes!

"Don't cry, Odelia," I said finally and with a touch of awkwardness, since I've never been particularly well-versed in the teachings of Elisabeth Kübler-Ross. For I had the strong suspicion someone had died and this is why my humans were in such an emotional state. But then I realized that if someone had died, it most probably was… Gran!

"Did something happen to Gran?" I asked therefore. "Did she… die?"

"Oh, Max," Odelia sniffled. "No, Gran is fine." And to prove it, she cried some more!

"We were very worried about you, Max," said Chase, proceeding to lift a part of the veil on why they were in this state. "Odelia actually thought something had happened to you, since her phone started beeping the moment your collar lost connection with you."

Finally understanding dawned. "Oh," I said, as I patted my human on the head. "I'm so sorry. I didn't think about that."

"Of course you didn't, Max," said Odelia, now smiling through her flood of tears, which was a strange sight indeed, and for a mere feline like myself very hard to interpret, I can tell you. Was she crying? Or was she smiling? Was she sad? Or was she happy? Tough!

"Look, I'm fine, you guys," I said, and got up from the bed to demonstrate my physical prowess. Of course, as I turned a few rounds, I accidentally slipped off the bed and tumbled to the floor, fortunately landing on all fours. It caused ripples of laughter to emanate from my humans, and I must confess I liked this a lot better. It's not much fun to realize you've caused pain and heartache, just by the inadvertent act of throwing off your collar, even though I still thought doing so had saved my life from those pesky kids.

"The kids who were chasing you," said Odelia, indicating she must have read my mind, "actually thought you were a hologram. Part of the Mokemon universe."

"Mokemon stands for Mock Monsters," Chase said. "It's an online game."

"They didn't realize they were chasing an actual cat until we told them."

"Dumb kids," Chase grumbled, showing me he wasn't as forgiving as Odelia when it came to youthful foolishness.

"But they made up for it," Odelia continued, "by helping us search for you. Of course we didn't find you, and that only made me even more worried."

I took a deep breath, and decided to tell all, and leave out no detail, however small, in an effort to place Odelia in full possession of the facts pertaining to the case. "I was kidnapped by Johnny and Jerry," I said, "but then Johnny had a change of heart and released me from the vehicle."

"Kidnapped!" cried Odelia, causing Chase to frown in consternation.

"Yeah, they thought they would exchange me for the George Calhoun film," I explained. "And even before that we saw several people burgle the house next door, but then you know all about that already." What she didn't know was that we'd overheard the paparazzo inform his employer about his efforts to obtain the film, and Tammy's husband calling home to apprise her of same.

Odelia dutifully translated my tale to her husband, who thoughtfully rubbed his formidable chin. "This is getting out of hand, babe," he said finally.

"Yeah, I think it's time we returned that film to George. Which reminds me—we should probably pay the guy a visit in the morning, seeing as he didn't show up."

Just then, Dooley came wandering into the room, looking glum and dejected. But then he caught sight of me, and his face cleared. He came tripping up to me and then he was hugging me and pressing me to his bosom, and crying, "Max! Oh, Max, there you are!"

"Yeah, I was never anywhere else," I said, once more surprised that as I'd lain there resting peacefully, apparently people and cats alike had missed me.

And then Dooley burst into a flood of tears, too! "I

thought something had happened to you, Max. I thought those kids had caught you for sure, and were doing all kinds of horrible things to you! And we looked for you everywhere, but when we couldn't find you, we figured we were too late, and Harriet was already thinking about your funeral, and said she wanted to be the one to deliver the eulogy, and Brutus said he wanted to carry the coffin, and and and..."

"I'm fine, Dooley," I said as I patted my friend on the back, same way I'd patted my human on the head. "I managed to escape those annoying kids."

"Oh, Max," said Dooley, and now he was laughing, and crying, and doing both at the same time, just like Odelia!

It was the weirdest thing.

And then when Brutus and Harriet came in, and saw me, the whole scene played out once again, with me explaining what had happened, and Harriet telling me all about the eulogy she was thinking of delivering, and looking a little disappointed that now she wasn't going to be able to go in front of the entire congregation and deliver it, and Brutus said he'd practiced how to carry my coffin by pressing his shoulder into a log of wood, and how happy he was he wouldn't have to carry my coffin, for that log of wood had hurt his shoulder and couldn't Odelia give him a nice shoulder rub now if she pleased?

It all ended with Odelia and Chase and the four of us finally settling down on the bed.

"What a day," said Harriet as she closed her eyes.

"You can say that again," said Brutus as he massaged his shoulder.

"Good night, Max," said Dooley happily.

"Good night, Dooley," I said.

"Good night, Harriet," said Dooley.

"Good night, Dooley."

"Good night, Brutus."

"Good night, Dooley. Good night, Max. Good night, Harriet."

"Good night, Max," said Harriet. "Good night, Odelia. Good night, Chase."

"Good night, babe," said Chase, fluffing up his pillow. "Good night, cats."

"Good night, babe," said Odelia. "Good night, you guys."

"Good night, Odelia," said Dooley. "Good night, Chase. Good night—"

"Oh, enough already!" I said.

I mean, seriously?

20

The next morning, we weren't awakened by the sound of birdsong, or even by the rays of sun peeking in through the window and making our eyelids flutter, but by that infernal phone. It rang incessantly, and with an insistence that was hard to ignore.

And so Odelia, who'd gone to bed very late last night, due to certain events I've painstakingly described in a previous chapter of these chronicles, reached out a hand, made a grab for the phone, and finally managed on the third try.

"Who is it?" asked Chase groggily.

Odelia, who always has trouble focusing before she's had her first cup of coffee, said, "Lemme just…" She frowned at the display, and finally murmured, "My uncle. I'll call him later."

And soon peace returned. We all went back to sleep, until ten seconds later Chase's phone chimed out the same tune— Odelia and Chase, ever since they got married, have matching ringtones: *Say You, Say Me* by Lionel Richie. Chase grabbed for his phone, checked the display, and said," Your uncle again."

"Better pick up," Odelia said, without moving an inch from her relaxed position on the pillow.

Chase heaved a tired groan, then put the phone to his ear. "Chief, what's up?" He listened for a moment, then a look of alarm came over him, and I could actually see life returning to his placid features as the man sat up a little straighter while listening to his commanding officer's voice. "I'll be there as soon as possible," he finally intoned. "Yeah, Odelia, too," he added as he glanced to the inert form next to him.

From the tousled head of hair, the disembodied voice of Odelia spoke. "What's going on?"

"George Calhoun is missing," said Chase as he immediately got out of bed and headed to the bathroom for that all-important first moment of the day: a hot shower.

"Missing? What do you mean, missing?"

"His wife called 911 this morning!" Chase called out from the bathroom. "Says George didn't come home last night, and when she woke up this morning, and he still wasn't there, she called all of his friends, and they all said they haven't seen him either."

"Oh, heck," Odelia groaned.

I lifted my head and found myself glancing into Dooley's lively eyes. He clearly was wide awake. "Looks like we've got a case, Max," he said, looking happy and relaxed. He then gave me a sweet smile. "I'm so happy you're not dead, Max."

"Please, Dooley. Let's not talk about that anymore. It frankly gave me the creeps."

"I'm glad you're not dead too, Max," said Harriet as she yawned and stretched. "Though I was really looking forward to delivering that eulogy. I had some great ideas Maybe I can still use them—next time you die, I mean."

"There won't be a next time, Harriet," I said.

"Why, are you planning to live forever?" asked Brutus with a grin.

"Yes, Brutus," I said. "I'm going to live forever, so you won't have to carry my coffin and hurt your shoulder."

"Oh, don't be like that, buddy," said Brutus, giving me a hearty slap on the back that made me topple straight off the bed and onto the carpet below. "I consider it an honor to carry your coffin. Of course they only asked me since I'm such a big strong cat. Dooley here wouldn't be able to even lift your coffin."

I stared at my friend. "And why is that, pray tell?"

"Because you're so darn heavy!" said the cat, not beating about the bush. He gave me a wink. "Must be those big bones of yours, huh?"

And here I thought today was going to be great day!

At least I had one thing going for me: now that Brutus had hurt his shoulder he'd decided to postpone my training regimen. Though he assured me that he was a fast healer, and as soon as he was feeling fine, we'd hit the track full steam! I have no idea what track he was referring to, but it sounded ominous. Track rhymes with rack, after all.

I still decided to start my day, hoping things would improve, but when I arrived downstairs, I discovered my bowl was empty. Odelia, in last night's melee, had forgotten to fill it. In fact all of our bowls were empty. And when I stepped into my litter box, I discovered it hadn't been cleaned out, and that the donations I'd made last night were still very much in evidence. And then finally, when I decided to go out, and through sheer force of habit took the short route through the pet flap, I found that in spite of yesterday's strenuous activity, I hadn't lost an inch of width, for promptly I got stuck—again!

Yep. It was one of those days where you probably are better off staying in bed!

Lucky for me Odelia didn't have time to bother with oil

or soap or whatever. Instead, she curtly said, "Chase, Max is stuck again. Give him a nudge, will you?"

"Sure thing, babe," I heard Chase say, and moments later I felt a powerful force applying pressure to my rear, and I was promptly propelled out of the pet flap, described a nice clean arc straight through the air, and dropped into a crumpled heap on the lawn.

"Thanks, babe," I heard Odelia say.

"No sweat, babe," Chase returned.

Yep, it was one of those days, all right!

$\mathcal{W}$e were driving in Chase's squad car, with the man himself behind the wheel, Odelia riding shotgun, and the four of us in the back, when I decided that maybe now was a good time to broach the subject I'd been thinking about since the day before. "Odelia?" I said.

"Mh?" said my human, who was intently studying George Calhoun's Wikipedia page.

"About that pet flap."

"What about it?"

"So I talked to Kingman yesterday, and he told us—"

"Listen to this, babe," said Odelia. "'George Calhoun has been known to suffer from fits of depression, most importantly in the early nineties, when his career wasn't going the way he hoped, and he later confessed in an interview with *Variety* that he'd been on the verge of taking his own life.'" She turned to her husband. "Do you think maybe the pressure of knowing that film is out there, and his wife knows, made him do something foolish?"

"Let's hope not," said Chase. "I like George. Always have. From the time he was a TV star."

"Okay, so about that pet flap," I tried again, after silence had descended upon the car once more. "So Kingman showed us something Wilbur installed for him. It's pretty cool."

"My mom and dad should never have told Anna," said Odelia, shaking her head.

"It was very hard not to, babe," said Chase.

"I know, but it should have been George, not my dad, who told her what was going on."

"Let's not start the blame game before we know what we're dealing with here."

"Fair enough," said our human.

Silence once more reigned supreme, and I saw my chance to broach a topic that was very near and dear to my heart, and my expanding midsection. "So about that pet flap…"

"Oh, stop it, Max!" Harriet snapped. "Can't you see that Odelia has other things to worry about right now than that stupid pet flap of yours?"

And so I decided to keep my trap shut—as shut as that pet flap was to me. It was obvious no one was even remotely interested in the predicament I found myself in: a life now stretched out before my mind's eye of incessant dieting, or else of Chase putting his sturdy foot against my rear end and shoving me through the pet flap at every opportunity.

Not a fun prospect!

We arrived at the large mansion where George Calhoun lives, only one of the many homes he calls his own. I've heard he has another house in Los Angeles, one in England, where he spends a lot of time with his wife, who's British-born, and also one in Italy, where he likes to spend his summers hanging out with his many famous friends. And as the car zoomed up the long drive, finally the picturesque Calhoun home hove into view: it was neatly bedecked with ivy, and looked like many of the fine mansions I've been privileged to be invited to in the course of a long and checkered sleuthing career.

Chase parked in the driveway, right next to a Range Rover, a Tesla and a Lamborghini, and as we got out, Anna came walking up to us. "Oh, Detective," she said as she placed a hand on Chase's arm, watched on by a frowning Odelia. "I'm so glad you're here. I'm frantic with worry. When George didn't come home last night, I thought he might be staying with a friend, but when I still hadn't heard from him this morning, I knew something was wrong." She touched her abdomen, and said, "A woman knows, Detective. And I simply know that something terrible must have happened to my husband."

We walked around the house, and soon found ourselves on a terrace, with a nice view of a large pool, and as I stared at the spot George had entertained his neighbor's wife not so long ago, Anna Calhoun gestured to that same pool with a sweep of her lovely arm.

"Here is where I saw him last. We had a flaming row, as you can imagine. I told him I knew what he'd done. That I'd seen the film. And what did he have to say for himself. And he said he didn't have to defend himself. That he was a grown man, and that marriage wasn't a golden cage but a voluntary bond between a man and a woman. Of course a lot of very harsh words followed, but then suddenly the twins came walking out of the house—in spite of our attempt to keep our voices down they must have heard the row, and wanted to know what was wrong. So I put them to bed again, and then I announced to George I was going to sleep, and that he could spend the night in the guest room or even go to hell for all I cared." She gave us a rueful look. "And that's the last time I saw him."

"Did he sleep in the guest bedroom?" asked Odelia.

Anna glanced over to Odelia, and frowned, as if wondering who she was.

Chase felt compelled to introduce her. "This is my wife Odelia—police consultant."

Anna glanced over to the house, where in one of the upstairs windows now the blond heads of two little boys had appeared, who were waving at us. But then what was probably a nanny intervened and pulled them back from the window, even as Anna absentmindedly returned their wave. "I think so," she said finally. "I haven't checked. Do you want to see the bedroom now? Maybe you can find some lead."

Chase gratefully accepted, and he and Odelia followed Anna into the house, while the four of us decided to stay put and take in the expansive scene.

"I think I'd like to live in a house like this," said Harriet as she tested the nice lawn with her paw. "So much space."

"Yeah, and look at those rose bushes over there, smoochie poo," said Brutus, indicating some lush and gorgeous-looking rose bushes. He wiggled his eyebrows meaningfully. "Wanna go check 'em out?"

At home, the rose bushes in Odelia's backyard are Harriet and Brutus's favorite place to rest and... do other stuff. And as we watched on, a giggling Harriet and a smirking Brutus now made a beeline for George Calhoun's rose bushes and soon sounds of the frolicking lovers could be heard.

I cleared my throat, and told my friend, "Let's take a look around, Dooley. Maybe we'll find some trace of George."

Dooley had walked up to the pool and stood staring at the clear blue water. "I thought for sure George would be floating in the pool," he said. "But he's not."

"Why would George be floating in the pool?" I asked as I joined my friend at the edge of the water. I dipped my paw in and found that it was of a very pleasant temperature.

"Because these Hollywood people are often found dead floating in pools."

"Not that often, Dooley," I said. "You make it sound as if it's their favorite pastime."

"Well, it is," he insisted. "Remember that John Paul George case, Max? He was found floating in his pool. And there have been others."

I agreed that floating in pools seems like a very pleasant way to pass the time for many a celebrity, but since this pool was completely devoid of Georges, we decided to try a different tack, and soon were wandering around the man's vast property. Most of it was smooth lawn, which was very pleasant under our paws, but at the edge of his property we found what looked like a miniature golf course, and lo and behold: a naked young man was playing a round of golf there. And if I say naked I mean he was wearing boxers, fortunately, and was none other than Chuck Crush, once more crossing our path.

"Oh, hiya, fellas," said Chuck when he caught sight of us. He was a little inebriated, as the smell of his breath told me, but otherwise he looked in fine fettle. "George asked me to meet him here," he announced. "But he stood me up." He shook his head. "I should have known he would. That's just the kind of guy he is."

"And why would you say that?" I asked.

"He can't help it, you know," said Chuck, continuing what in his view was probably a monologue. "Ever since he got married he hasn't been the same. Used to be we would hang out together all the time. Get drunk in bars and pick up girls on the Strip. Or fly to Hawaii for the weekend and get drunk and fly back on Monday morning to go rock climbing in the Rocky Mountains, just the two of us." He heaved a sad sigh as he hit a ball with his club. "Those days are long gone. He's become a 'family man,'" he said, making air quotes. "All he can think about is Anna and the kids. But his oldest, closest friend? He doesn't give a hoot about me anymore." He shrugged. "So I hang around, hoping against hope that he'll remember me. Remember the good old days. At least he lets me live above his garage, so there's that. And he does visit me from time to time to see how I'm doing."

"He doesn't seem very happy, Max," said Dooley, referring to the semi-naked actor.

"No, he certainly doesn't," I agreed.

"Do you think he had something to do with George's disappearance?"

"I don't know, Dooley. It's too soon to tell."

"I told him only last night, 'George,' I said," said Chuck, slurring his words a little, "'if you want me gone, I'm gone. Just say the word.' But he said, 'No, Chuck. I need you. My marriage is on the rocks, my life is a mess, and you're the only one I can talk to.' So I told him that maybe that was a good thing. That he wasn't cut out for the life of a married man, same as me. But of course George found the whole thing very hard. Said he loves Anna. And how stupid he was. And could I maybe talk to her?" He produced a soft laugh. "As if Anna would listen to me. That woman hates my guts! Always has. She sees me as a remnant of George's past—the scabrous George. George the rogue. Wild George the ladies' man!"

He blinked and directed his club at that little white ball again. This time he missed and the club swung too far, and he ended up accidentally hitting himself in the head some-how. He went cross-eyed for a moment, then before our very eyes keeled over.

"Is he dead, Max?" asked Dooley.

"Um…" I said, then gave the world-famous actor a gentle

poke in his sixpack. "I don't think so," I said finally, when I saw his chest go up and down. "He's just unconscious."

"Oh, good. Imagine Brutus having to carry this guy's coffin."

I gave my friend a strange look, then said, "We better tell Odelia to call an ambulance."

22

While Chase was on the phone with the emergency services so they could send an ambulance, Odelia was still engaged with Anna Calhoun. The two ladies had found a nice place to conduct the interview in the greenhouse, with plenty of exotic flowers to keep them company. Anna had created for herself a cozy spot in the back of the greenhouse, where she said she liked to spend a lot of her time, reading and working, surrounded by all that lush green. It relaxed her, she said. Something that was necessary for one who had made a name for herself as a staunch defender of the rights of minorities the world over.

"Did you threaten George with divorce?" asked Odelia. She'd taken a seat directly across from Anna, who sat in what I assumed was her usual spot, on a chaise longue, where I could picture her lying down, working diligently on the defense of her next client.

Anna's sleek dark hair had fallen across her face like a curtain, and she now tucked it behind one ear. "I may have used the D word, I don't remember. You have to understand that I was extremely upset when I found out about that film, and even more so after I'd watched it. So I told George a few home truths, about the sanctity of marriage, about the value of his wedding vows, and about the twins, and what they would think when they inevitably find out at some point in their lives what kind of man their father is."

"And what did he say?"

"He exhausted himself in explanations and apologies, as was to be expected. But I told him he could stick his apologies and his explanations where the sun doesn't shine." She leveled a steady look at Odelia. "Men are creatures of habit, Mrs. Kingsley."

"Odelia, please."

"And it's not as if I wasn't warned. All my friends told me when I met George that a man like him isn't marriage material. George's reputation is well established, and precedes him: the man often boasted about the number of women he has slept with. He was the epitome of the staunch bachelor. The man who vowed he'd never marry, never be tied down, for whom the idea of raising a family was the worst thing that could happen to any man. He lived with a duck, for crying out loud, and so when we started dating, all of my friends, and my family, told me I was crazy. That I was setting myself up for disaster."

"Do you think meeting you changed him?"

"I thought so," said Anna. "I really thought he'd changed. At least that's what he told me. He said he'd waited a long time for love to finally enter his life, but now that he found me, he wasn't letting go. And then when the twins were born, he said he'd never known how great marriage could be. He was a changed man, and I was the one who tamed him." She smiled at the memory. "Of course I thought that was wonderful. It stroked my ego. To think I was the only woman on the planet who'd managed to tame George, the ultimate bachelor."

"What did his friends think of all this?"

Anna's face clouded. "They weren't happy, I can tell you that. In fact they were furious. They saw me as some kind of monster, who was taking their friend away from them. And I won't lie: a lot of things changed for George, but even more so for his friends. No more all-night parties, no more trips to Vegas, no more boozing and whoremongering."

"What's whoremongering, Max?" asked Dooley.

"Um… well, let's just say it's spending time with a woman who isn't your wife, Dooley."

"You mean like when Chase spends time with Gran or Marge?"

"Not exactly," I said. But then Odelia asked her next question, and we both assumed our listening position once more.

"What about Chuck Crush?" asked Odelia.

"What about him?" asked Anna as her expression hardened.

"How did he feel about your marriage? He was George's best friend."

"Still is," said Anna. "Shortly after George got married, Chuck got married, too, and so for a while things were great. Both men seemed to have turned a corner, and we double-dated a couple of times, and when the twins were born, and then Chuck adopted the first of his kids, we organized play dates when they were old enough. Or Chuck or his wife would babysit the twins and vice versa."

"But then Chuck divorced."

"Then Chuck divorced," Anna said, nodding, "and that's when the trouble started. Chuck felt that now that he was single again, he wanted to make up for lost time, by throwing himself back into the dating game, and taking up his old partying ways again."

"And he expected George to join him."

"Even though he said he didn't, I think unconsciously he

was hoping that George would somehow join him, and the two of them could pick up where they left off. But of course George wasn't getting divorced, and he wasn't prepared to break up his family just so he could relive his younger years with Chuck as his wingman, just like the old days."

"And so Chuck was disappointed."

"Extremely disappointed."

"What is he doing here, if I may ask?"

"Honestly? I have no idea," said Anna with a laugh. "He arrived last month, and he hasn't left. He lives over the garage now, and it doesn't look like he ever intends to leave. And honestly, I think he's a bad influence on George. In fact since Chuck arrived, George has been hitting the nightlife pretty hard, even though he's ten years older now. So he's not having fun, and it makes him cranky because he realizes he's not as young as he was."

"Have you discussed this with him?"

"Oh, many times. I won't lie to you, Odelia, I don't like it —and I don't like it that Chuck is staying here. He's a disruptive presence in our lives. George has been spending a lot of time with Chuck, neglecting the twins... and me." She paused and studied her fingertips for a moment. "I think Chuck introduced George to Tammy Freiheit."

"Your neighbor."

Anna nodded. "She's very pretty, and not very faithful to her husband, and she and Chuck know each other." She looked up. "Did you know that Tammy and Chuck used to date?"

"No, I didn't know that."

"Well, they did. And now, apparently, Tammy is eager to get her claws into my George." She wiped away a small tear. "No, I'm not that woman's biggest fan, if you must know."

Chase entered the greenhouse, and rubbed his neck. "They've taken him to the hospital."

"Will he live?" asked Anna, and for a moment I had the impression there was a touch of wistfulness in her voice, as if she wouldn't mind if Chuck had hit his last golf ball.

"Oh, yeah," said Chase. "He managed to knock himself out, but he'll be just fine."

Odelia looked up at her hubby. "I think we better go and talk to Tammy," she said now.

"When you do," said Anna, getting up, "tell her that if she ever sets foot in my house again, I'll have her arrested for trespassing. I'm not kidding."

No, it certainly didn't look as if she was. Nor could I blame her.

23

J have to say that the house where Tammy and her husband lived wasn't nearly as nice and luxurious as the Calhoun place. It still was a great deal bigger than our house, though, but then that's not so difficult, since Odelia and Chase live in what is commonly termed a shoebox, with its one bedroom and one guest bedroom and tiny living room that also doubles as the kitchen and its small strip of green we like to call the backyard.

"Now this is what I call a backyard," said Brutus, who'd joined us again, after exploring those rose bushes to his heart's content. In fact I could detect a few rose petals in Harriet's fur, and she looked altogether too happy to be conducting what could very well be a murder investigation, since we still had no idea what had happened to George.

"So George has gone missing?" asked Tammy, who was dressed in a tank top that left nothing to the imagination. In fact I had the impression the concept of a bra was alien to her, as her assets were jiggling all over the place, and judging from the color that had seeped into Chase's cheeks, even that hardened cop was not entirely unaffected by Tammy's charm.

"Yes," said Odelia, regarding her hubby with a touch of censure. "He hasn't been seen since last night. So is he here?"

"No, he sure ain't," said Tammy, then reluctantly stepped aside to let us in. "Mark!" she bellowed. "It's the cops!"

Mark, who I recognized as the man who'd tried to burgle Gran's room last night, mistakenly seeing it as the potential source of films featuring his wife in a starring role with George Calhoun, didn't look all that impressed. "What do they want?" he grunted.

"George is missing," Tammy explained.

"So they think we might be hiding him or something?"

She shrugged. "I don't know why they'd think George would come here."

"If George ever sets foot in this house," said Mark, his voice taking on a harsher tone, "I'll kick him so hard he won't know what hit him."

Odelia shared a look of concern with her husband. "So when was the last time you saw your neighbor, Mr. Freiheit?"

"Why?" said Mark, reddening. "Are you accusing me of something? Huh?"

"Settle down, sir," said Chase, holding out his hands in an appeasing gesture. "We just want to ask you some questions."

"It's all right, sweetie," said Tammy. "These cops are just doing their job."

She led us into the living room, which was dominated by just about the biggest television screen I've ever seen. A NASCAR race was playing out on the screen, with the loud roar of the engines bouncing off the walls, where plenty of pictures of Tammy in flattering but unrevealing poses vied for space with pictures of NASCAR drivers and cars. Obviously Mark Freiheit only had two big loves in his life: his wife and NASCAR, and he had a hard time deciding which one of them he enjoyed more.

Odelia and Chase took a seat on the white leather couch and moments later Tammy returned with a tray with glasses of what looked like Coca Cola, complete with ice tinkling in those glasses, and as she set the tray down in front of Chase, there was so much jiggling and wiggling going on, that Chase's face now turned as red as Tammy's husband's.

"Honey, why don't you put on something more decent?" asked Mark.

"Why, isn't this decent enough for you?" asked Tammy as she placed her hands on two shapely hips. Apart from the tank top she was also clad in Daisy Dukes and not much more. Her hair was blond, her eyes wide and blue, and she looked like every hormonal teenager's dream girl, and probably also every not-so-hormonal man's dream woman.

Mark relented and Tammy took a seat next to him on the couch, giving Odelia and Chase an expectant look as she popped a piece of gum into her mouth and chewed it noisily.

"So I think we need to address the elephant in the room," said Odelia finally.

Tammy frowned. "What elephant? All I see is four cats."

Mark, who'd muted the television, now also frowned. "Yeah, I don't get it either."

"I think my wife is referring to the film of Tammy and George," said Chase.

Mark rolled his eyes. "Oh, that," he said.

"Look, George and I are adults," said Tammy. "And as adults, we just want to have some fun. There's no law against that, is there?"

"No, there certainly isn't," Odelia agreed. "Unless that fun involves a married man, who ends up disappearing two days later."

"Oh, please," said Tammy, rolling those expressive eyes of

hers. "I bet he and Anna had a fight over that silly video, and so George walked off on a huff."

"Yeah, he's probably in Vegas right now, sleeping off a bender," said Mark. "Have you checked the airports? That's what you should be doing right now, instead of harassing innocent people like Tammy and me."

"How do you feel about your wife engaging in these frivolous activities with your neighbor, Mr. Freiheit?" asked Chase.

Mark shrugged. "Like Tammy says, it's just some innocent fun between two consenting adults."

"You take a very liberal view of your wife's infidelities," said Odelia.

"When we got hitched we agreed on an open marriage. Besides, I know I'm the one she loves, and this thing with George, well, that was a one-time deal, wasn't it, sweetie?"

"Oh, absolutely," said Tammy. "I like George a lot, but Mark is my husband, and I wouldn't dream of leaving him."

"Do you think George would consider leaving Anna for you?"

Tammy thought about this for a moment, then shook her head. "I don't think so. At least he told me he wouldn't. And I don't think he was lying." She smiled and cocked her head. "I can tell when a man is lying, and George was definitely telling me the truth."

"Also, there's the twins," said Mark. "George wouldn't leave those kids over a fling."

"Oh, but it wasn't just a fling," said Tammy as she rubbed her husband's arm.

"Shut up, Tam," Mark said under his breath.

"Yes, Marky," said Tammy as she let go of her husband's bicep.

"You know what I think?" I said.

"That Tammy is very pretty?" Dooley asked.

"That, too. But I think this whole film business just might have been an opportunity for Mark and Tammy to make some extra money."

"What do you mean?" asked Harriet.

"Well, if Mark had gotten his hands on that film last night, he could have sold it back to George for a nice chunk of change. Or they could have decided to sell it to a producer, or to a website that specializes in that kind of thing, for a considerable price."

Odelia, who'd overheard me, now eyed Mark thoughtfully. "You were seen last night crawling through my grandmother's window, Mark. Can you please tell me what you were trying to accomplish? Or you, Tammy—breaking into Wilbur Vickery's home yesterday."

Mark blinked a few times, and had the decency to look embarrassed. "Well…"

"Call a lawyer, Marky," said Tammy.

"Um…" said her husband.

"Tell them we won't talk to them without a lawyer."

"It is your prerogative to engage the services of a lawyer," Chase confirmed, "but it will only serve to make you look more guilty."

"Even more guilty than you already are," said Odelia, "since a witness has formally identified you, Mr. Freiheit. Your mask dropped when you fell down that ladder," she added with a tight smile.

"Marky!" Tammy cried, and slapped her husband on the arm. "Now why did you have to go and do a stupid thing like that for!"

"How was I to know that old dame would hit me!" Mark grumbled. "It's a miracle I didn't break my neck when I fell down that ladder." Then he looked up and seemed to realize he'd just put himself in quite the predicament. "Oops."

"Look, my grandmother isn't pressing charges… yet," said

Odelia. "And neither is Wilbur, as far as I know. But we do need to know why you did this."

Mark rubbed his face. "Okay, all right," he said finally.

"Marky! Don't say another word!"

"Tam, they caught me red-handed!"

She glanced down at his hands. "Your hands look fine to me."

"Look, when I heard about that film, I just figured, why not strike the iron while it's hot, see?"

"Marky!"

"Will you just let me explain?"

Tammy folded her arms across her chest and looked the other way, clearly upset with her husband.

"So I thought, why not get my hands on that film and then sell it to one of those big smut publishers, you know? A tape with George Calhoun? That's the jackpot. George is a global star, and pretty much everyone would want to see that."

"He wasn't so hot, you know," said Tammy, rejoining the conversation. "I'd give him a solid five. Marriage has made that man soft—and I mean that literally."

"What is she talking about, Max?" asked Dooley.

"Pudgy," I said after a pause. "She's talking about George's pudgy midsection."

"Yeah, plenty of guys allow themselves to go soft around the midsection—and some cats, too," said Brutus with a meaningful look in my direction.

"So I wanted that film. Is that so bad?"

"No, unless you deliberately sent your wife in there to ensnare George and to film the scene yourself."

"Oh, and how would I have done that?" said Mark. "It's not as if I snuck a camera crew in there while Tammy was doing... what she was doing." He dragged a hand through his hair, and directed an unhappy look at his wife.

"You don't look very happy with Tammy's and George's escapades," said Odelia, adopting a more compassionate tone.

Mark shook his head. "That's because I'm not," he said, and suddenly choked up.

Tammy took hold of her hubby's arm again. "What is it, Marky?" she said. "I thought you said you didn't mind?"

"I lied," he said, still choky-voiced. "I don't like it when you do that kind of stuff, Tam. I really don't."

"Oh, huggy bear. Why didn't you tell me?"

"Because I thought I wouldn't mind—but now I find that I do."

"Oh, huggy bear! What are you saying?"

"Tam, won't you make an honest man out of me?"

"Marky!"

And suddenly, before our very eyes, suddenly Marky went down on one knee and said, "Tammy Freiheit, I know we're already married, but let's renew our vows, and this time let's can this open marriage business and start a family together—what do you say?"

"Oh, Marky!" said Tammy, then looked around, and when she couldn't find what she was looking for, a tiny frown marred her smooth brow. "No ring?" she finally asked.

"Don't you worry about that," said Mark. "I'll get you the biggest rock you've ever seen."

Tammy's face lit up again. "Oh, Marky."

And then the two were hugging it out, and hugging led to kissing, and for a moment it seemed as if they'd completely forgotten that they had an audience, until finally Chase cleared his throat, and they broke the kiss.

"Um…" said Mark, looking flustered, his hair mussed where Tammy had ruffled it. "So tell your granny I'm very sorry," he told Odelia.

"And tell her she can keep that video," said Tammy

happily as she clutched her man close now. "We won't be needing it anymore."

The interview seemed to have come to a most natural conclusion, and as Odelia and Chase rose to their feet, Odelia asked, "So you have no idea where George is?"

"No, and I don't care," said Tammy decidedly. And it didn't look like she was lying. In fact Tammy didn't look like the kind of person who was capable of telling a lie.

And so moments later we were outside again, allowing the soon-to-be (again) Mr. and Mrs. Freiheit to enjoy their post-proposal happiness. And as the door closed, we could hear the distinct sounds of the wedding march blasting through the living room speakers.

"Another dead end," said Chase.

"Yeah, but don't they look happy together?"

Chase smiled and then hugged his wife close and soon kissing ensued.

And when I glanced back, I saw that Harriet was giving Brutus loving nudges, too.

"Kissing is contagious, Max," said Dooley, who'd noticed the same phenomenon.

"Yeah, looks like," I said.

We still had no idea where George Calhoun was, though, and wasn't that the whole point of this investigation?

𝒲e were in the car, parked in front of Tammy and Mark's house, Odelia and Chase going through the case with the kind of cold logic that had served them so well in the past.

"Okay, so Tammy and Mark Freiheit," said Chase. "Motive: Mark was clearly upset with George for engaging in a brief affair with Tammy, and judging from the passion we just saw him display when he proposed, he loves that woman a lot, and presumably hates George just as much."

"I agree that Mark is a definite candidate to do away with George," said Odelia, as she jotted the man's name down on her list of suspects. "Next: Tammy."

"Tammy could have been upset with George when he decided he didn't want to pursue an affair with her and chose to stay with his wife instead," Chase suggested.

"Tammy Freiheit," said Odelia as she jotted the woman's name down.

"And then there's Anna, of course. I don't think we need to discuss her motive."

"Anna Calhoun," Odelia said as she wrote down George's wife's name.

"There's also that paparazzo," I said. "So eager to get his hands on that film that he decided to break in last night. It's possible he and George met, they argued, and the paparazzo struck George."

"Paparazzo," said Odelia, writing this down.

"And let's not forget about Johnny and Jerry," said Harriet. "They did try to catnap Max last night."

"But why would they hurt George?" asked Odelia.

"Same thing as with the paparazzo. It's possible they met, or that George was on his way to us to pick up that film, as promised, and he bumped into those two instead. An argument ensued—"

"Or they decided to kidnap the guy," said Brutus.

"Okay, so Johnny and Jerry go on the list," said Odelia, and then proceeded to enlighten Chase, who'd been waiting patiently for all that caterwauling to finally stop.

"Our list of suspects is getting longer and longer," said the cop, "but we still have no idea what happened to George. Whether he's dead or alive—or drunk in a ditch."

"Maybe if we talk to all these people," said Odelia, tapping her list, "we'll find him."

"So who do you want to talk to first?" asked Chase as he clicked his seatbelt into place.

Just then, who would park their car in front of us but Johnny and Jerry themselves!

Chase quirked an eyebrow at Odelia, who responded by quirking an eyebrow at him, and we all got out of the car.

The moment the two crooks caught sight of us, Jerry threw up his hands in a gesture of utter frustration. "For crying out loud—what is it this time!"

"Hi, Odelia," said Johnny. "Hi, Chase. And look at those

149

little cuties," he added as he crouched down and tickled me under my chin.

"Will you leave those stupid beasts alone!" his partner cried.

"They're not beasts, Jer. They're very clever pussies. Aren't you, buddy? Aren't you?"

"Yes, I am a very clever pussy, Johnny," I said, quickly tiring of this baby talk.

"Did you see that, Jer!" said Johnny excitedly. "He just talked back to me!"

"Great," Jerry grumbled. "Now what do you want, Detective?"

"You broke into my in-laws' house last night," said Chase. "And not for the first time either. This time I guess you were looking for the Calhoun film. So I'm going to ask this once, and if I like your answer, I'm going to let your attempted burglary slide. If I don't, I'm going to arrest you and throw your asses in jail."

Jerry seemed to swallow away a lump, for his Adam's apple bobbed up and down engagingly. The man had never looked more like a ferret than he did now, but he also looked like a scared ferret. A ferret who knows that the gig is up.

"Shoot," he finally managed to say.

"Did either of you by any chance run into George last night?"

"And did you, after you tried to grab Max, abduct George instead?" asked Odelia sternly.

Jerry blinked, then said, "I have no idea what—"

"Uh-uh," said Chase, wagging a reproachful finger.

"Okay, all right! So we did try to get our hands on that film."

"We heard your dad had it," Johnny explained, "so we figured we might as well grab it."

"But unfortunately we went in through the wrong

window—for which I still blame you, Johnny," he added, poking a bony finger in his partner's chest.

"It wasn't my fault, Jer! They must have switched rooms!"

"Or you switched brains," Jerry grumbled. "Anyway, we didn't get the film, and we didn't abduct Max either, since animal lover here let him get away."

"But you did grab him," said Odelia, and this time she looked positively irate.

"Okay, so I shouldn't have done it!" said Jerry. "It was one of those spur-of-the-moment ideas. We saw him running away from some kids, so we decided to help him make his getaway. And then when he was in the car, I suddenly had this bright idea that we might use him for leverage. Only Johnny put a stop to that, didn't you?" he added with some vehemence, indicating not all was well in this particular partnership.

"You don't abduct people's pets, Jer," said Johnny adamantly. "You just don't."

"Thank you for that, Johnny," said Odelia, but kept giving Jerry the evil eye, showing me she really did care, even if she forgot to fill my bowl, or forgot to clean out my litter box, or didn't listen when I tried to apprise her of a new and improved type of pet flap.

"Okay, so here's my final question," said Chase, "and I want you to think long and hard before you give me an answer: did you grab George Calhoun last night?"

Jerry immediately said, "Are you kidding? I wish! I mean," he quickly added, "no, we didn't, Detective Kingsley."

"I've never met George," said Johnny, "but if I did, I'd tell him I really like his movies. Especially the old ones, though. The ones he made as a director are all pretty terrible."

"Okay," said Chase, "I believe you."

"I'm telling you the truth," said Jerry. "Like I always do.

Since I found religion I haven't been able to tell a single lie. Now how weird is that, huh?"

"Sure," said Chase, then placed his hand on the man's shoulder and escorted him back to his car. "Now I think it's time for you to get lost, Vale. You, too, Carew."

"Oh, but we will, Detective," said Jerry. "We'll get as lost as you like."

"Say hi to your mom, Odelia," said Johnny. "And Scarlett."

"I will," said Odelia. "And try to stay on the straight and narrow from now on, will you?"

Johnny glanced over to his partner, who was fussing with the car seat, bucking back and forth and trying to move it closer to the steering wheel. "I would," he said. "But it's much harder for Jerry than it is for me." He dropped his voice to a conspiratorial whisper. "I think what he needs is the love of a good woman. It makes all the difference." And with these surprisingly wise words, he also got into the car, having to duck down his head to fit, and gave us a wave as they took off.

"I have a feeling we haven't seen the last of those two," said Odelia.

"I have a feeling you're right," said Chase. And then as he glanced across the road, suddenly he caught sight of another potential suspect, taking plenty of pictures of the front of George's house, and of Anna as she emerged in her car, possibly to go shopping in town.

Immediately the cop crossed the road with long-legged and determined steps, and grabbed the paparazzo by the collar before the man could skedaddle.

"And now it's between you and me," Chase growled as the man let out a surprised shriek.

$\mathcal{W}$hile Chase interviewed his next suspect, I let the events of the last couple of days pass through my mind, and let my little gray cells process them in the order they'd transpired. And when Odelia joined her husband to talk to the paparazzo, there was one thing that stood out in my mind: George, though a staunch and convinced bachelor before his wedding, had in the last couple of years proven himself a devoted family man. Okay, so he made a mistake getting involved with Tammy, but I was pretty sure he was sorry.

And as I thought of the interviews Odelia and Chase had conducted, one thing stood out to me: that sometimes when a man reaches a certain age, that man suddenly goes a little crazy, and decides to try and recapture his so-called freedom and the joys of an ill-spent youth. He soon comes to regret this, especially a man like George, who'd emerged from these interviews as a man who'd really changed his ways, probably feeling terrible when faced with the anger of the spouse he adores, and ended up… where, exactly?

Well, that was pretty obvious, wasn't it?

*G*eorge Calhoun opened his eyes and immediately wished he hadn't, for the most terrible pain sliced through his poor head. He recognized that pain, and in fact welcomed that pain, for it meant that A) he was still alive and B) he hadn't digested last night's bender to end all benders as well as he'd hoped.

He opened his eyes again, and this time groaned when that same sharp pain cut through him like a knife, but now at least he took the time to study his surroundings.

He was in a strange bed in a strange room, but was happy to note that at least he wasn't in the company of another Tammy Freiheit.

Thank God for small favors, he thought as he carefully removed the sheet that was twisted around him and checked if he was still in one piece. He was in a hotel room, and now remembered how he'd flown out to Vegas two nights ago, after that terrible row with Anna, and ended up trying to soak up all the alcohol on the Strip and failed miserably.

What no sportsman ever seems to understand is that there is always more alcohol in the world than his liver will be able to process. And in fact it was George's poor liver that now loudly protested against the treatment he'd given it.

He glanced over to the nightstand, in search of his phone, and when he didn't find it, remembered he'd tossed it into the fountain in front of Caesars Palace last night, in a foolish act of rebellion.

The best thing that ever happened to him was Anna and the twins, and he'd thrown it all away for a meaningless fling with a hot neighbor. Hadn't he learned anything?

He struggled to get up, but had to wait for the room to stop spinning, and the contents of his stomach to decide whether to come up or stay down. Both matters settled to his satisfaction, he shuffled into the bathroom, found what he was looking for in the form of some aspirin, and immediately downed one with some water from the tap and sank down on the toilet seat, waiting for the miracle of pharmacology to start spreading its joy through his ravaged system.

And as he shuffled out of the bathroom again, and dropped down on the bed, he wondered what the rest of his life would look like, now that Anna had told him in no uncertain terms how she viewed the state of their marriage: the same way he felt his middle-aged body was in: not too good!

And as he thought somber thoughts about his non-existent future, which seemed filled with plenty of Tammys and no Annas or the twins, he tumbled into a deep sleep once more, and was soon oblivious to the insistent knocking on his hotel room door.

&.

*W*hen George woke up again, his head was hurting a lot less already. He still felt as if the bottom had fallen out of the world, and the room was still spinning when he tried to open his eyes, and that same feeling of nausea still washed over him, but at least he didn't feel as if a man with a blunt ax was standing over him, trying to split his head in two.

There did seem to be a man hitting him with a hammer, though, but when he finally became aware of his surroundings, he realized it wasn't his head the man was banging with that hammer, but the poor door.

And as he watched on, suddenly the door flew open, and a procession of people stumbled in. First there was a smallish man with a mustache, who could only be the manager of the establishment he'd decided to grace with his patronage.

Behind him, a large and burly man appeared, who looked to be all muscle and hard surfaces. Even his face seemed made up of muscle and not much else. He was regarding him with a stern expression, as if George had personally offended him, though as far as he could tell, he'd never met him before. Had he beaten the guy at poker last night? Was he a mob enforcer?

Next was a fair-haired woman, small and thin, who regarded him with more compassion than he felt he deserved after having behaved like such a terrible cad. And then, much to his surprise, suddenly Anna appeared, accompanied by no less than four cats. And it was the cats that cinched the deal: he now realized he was still fast asleep, and this was all a dream. So he closed his eyes again, and went right back to sleep.

He woke up when a soft hand touched his cheek, and an even softer voice penetrated the haze that lay across his mind like a shroud, and then cold wetness seeped into his scalp. He frowned, for he'd recognized that voice as belonging to the great love of his life, and as he glanced up into her eyes, he couldn't believe how lovingly she gazed upon him. The big muscular fellow had placed a cold towel on his head and was now squeezing it, causing cold water to run across his face. He still looked like a mob enforcer, though.

The cats were still there, and he now considered they might be real, just like the rest.

"Anna?" he finally said, his voice hoarse, his mouth dry.

"George, honey, I've been so worried about you."

"You were?"

"Of course."

He was so happy to hear that, that he actually teared up. But then he became aware of the mob enforcer staring down at him with that stony look of a killer in his eyes.

"Can you please tell Captain Beefcake to stop sloshing water all over me?"

"This is Chase Kingsley, and he's a cop," said Anna, still stroking his head tenderly. "And that's Odelia. They're the ones who tracked you down."

"They did, did they?" he said, giving the twosome not the world's friendliest look. "So what if I didn't want to be tracked down? What if I wanted to wallow here in pain?"

"They figured that a man who's in love with his wife, but did a very foolish thing that hurt her deeply, might feel so bad about himself that he would return to his old stomping ground. And what better place to find you than here, the place you called your second home before you ended up with me."

"The day I ended up with you was the best day of my life," said George fervently. "Only that's all over now. You're going to divorce me and I'll end up the dumb schmuck who threw away the best thing that ever happened to him. And I've got no one to blame but myself."

"Is that really what you think?"

"Which part?"

"The part where I'm the best thing that ever happened to you."

"Of course! Only I was an idiot, wasn't I? Fooling around with that blond bombshell."

There was a slight diminution of endearment in Anna's facial expression, and he realized that if he was going to prostrate himself before her and express how sorry he was, he was going to have to up his game considerably.

"Tammy means nothing to me, honey. I guess I had one of those attacks of stupidity, there's no other word for it. So when Chuck introduced me to Tammy…"

"Oh, so Chuck introduced you, did he?" There was definitely some fire in her eyes now.

"He did. He and Tammy used to date, and when he bumped into her at a party in town, and discovered we were neighbors, he suggested we all hang out together."

"Oh, he did, did he?"

"He sure did. And so we did hang out, but then Chuck left, and then it was just Tammy and me, and I must confess I'd had a little too much to drink, so when she suddenly started kissing me all over the place, I should have stopped her right there and then." He sighed. "And that I didn't, is something I'll regret for the rest of my life. Which, judging from the terrible headache I have right now, might be very soon." He gazed up at her. "Can I have another aspirin, you think?"

"First you need to tell me something, George," said Anna, and suddenly the cheek-stroking and the loving kindness stopped, as if turned off at the tap.

"What is it?" he asked in a small voice.

"If I decide to take you back—and mind you, that's a very big if—will this ever happen again?"

"No, absolutely not," he said immediately, and he meant it, too.

"How can I be sure?"

"Because there's no one I love more than you, sweetness," said George. "You're worth a thousand Tammys to me, a million Tammys." There was plenty of other good stuff he could have said, but his brain wasn't working so well right then, and as he tried to rally his thoughts, and launch into an impassioned speech, suddenly she grabbed him by the ears and pressed a kiss to his lips that made him forget all about his headache. And when finally she broke the kiss, he blinked and said, "Does that mean you forgive me?"

"I do," she said warmly, "but only on one condition."

"Anything."

"You're going to tell Chuck to get lost."

"Consider him gone."

"And you'll never speak to Tammy again."

"Never."

"And for Pete's sakes, George, next time you have one of these midlife crises, try to be a little less cliché about it, will you?"

"Next time I have a midlife crisis," he said with a smile, "which won't happen, of course."

"It better not."

"I'll take up smoking instead. Nice, big, fat cigars."

"Please don't."

"Just kidding, sweetheart."

And as he glanced down, attracted by a strange sound, he saw four cats intently staring up at him, a small gray one meowing approvingly. And he could have been mistaken, but it was almost as if the cat was saying, 'Way to go, whoremonger!'

EPILOGUE

I stared at my pet flap and thought about what could have been, but what now looked as if it never would. I'd finally been able to explain to Odelia about Kingman's sophisticated, high-tech pet flap, the Pet Funnel 5000, and had even told her this was the pet flap to end all pet flaps—in other words, the pet flap of the future and beyond.

But it had all been to no avail. She'd said that if I wanted to fit through the pet flap, I simply had to start eating less, and that was her final word about the matter.

I'd even talked to Gran, and had given her the same spiel, but the old lady and Odelia had clearly talked to each other, and had decided to form a united front, and so even Gran had told me I needed to take my dieting more seriously, since no one likes a fat cat.

And so after throwing a final glance at the pet flap, I tucked in my belly, took one step in its direction, closed my eyes and moved through. And lo and behold: I didn't get stuck!

And as I moved through it a second time, just to make

sure the first time hadn't been a fluke, I was greeted with a big surprise when I found my entire family all waiting there for me: Odelia and Chase were there, but also Marge and Tex, Gran and Uncle Alec, and even Charlene and Scarlett, the more recent editions to the Poole clan. And of course my best friends Dooley, Harriet and Brutus.

They were all cheering me on loudly, as if I'd just finished a marathon, and I must say they weren't far from the truth, for it had cost me a lot of effort to fit through the flap again.

I'd cut down on my eating, and Brutus had put me through my paces by making me put in ten laps around the block every morning and every night. And it showed, for my belly had definitely shrunk, though now it kinda hung, its volume replaced by flabby skin. I needed to talk to Odelia about a nip and a tuck, but that was for a later date.

And as I wiped away a tear, Dooley was the first to come up and congratulate me.

"Well done, Max," he said.

"I knew you had it in you, buddy," said Brutus, as he gave me a hearty slap on the back.

"I think you'll find that you'll feel much better now, Max," said Harriet.

"I do feel much better," I admitted. "I have more energy, and I'm not out of breath when I climb the stairs."

"You even sing better," said Brutus, but then grinned. "Just kidding!"

Well, kidding or not, I did feel better, and I hadn't even needed that collar to get me there, either.

And as we all moved next door, where Tex's grill was already producing the kind of smoke to rival the likes of Chernobyl, and the humans all took a seat around the table, with the four of us to make ourselves comfortable on the porch swing, Odelia relayed the events as they'd transpired in Vegas for the umpteenth time to the rest of the family. It isn't every day that you're present at the reunion of a world-famous movie star and his wife, of course, and it isn't every day either that they invite you to the renewal of their wedding vows either. Even us cats were all invited, which was probably a first.

"So do you think George will keep his hands to himself next time he meets a voluptuous blonde?" asked Gran as she accepted a reasonably decent-looking sausage from her son-in-law.

"I don't think he'll ever do it again," said Chase.

"No," said Odelia. "You should have seen the look on his face. He loves his wife."

"I wish I'd been there," said Marge, who is a true romantic at heart.

"And I wish I'd seen that film before you destroyed it," said Scarlett. And when all eyes turned to her, she added, "What? Who hasn't dreamed of watching George in action?"

"Not me," Marge murmured quickly.

"Me neither," said Charlene.

"Or me," said Odelia.

"Liars," said Scarlett with an indulgent smile.

"I saw the footage and I have to say I was disappointed," said Gran. "The guy's got a dad bod!" she added when the others all made protesting noises.

"He's got a dad bod because he is a dad," said Marge. "And being a dad, he probably should make sure he doesn't allow himself to get in such a compromising position ever again." And then she patted her hubby's arm. "And you should make sure never to shoot such a video, honey."

"Oh, I won't," Tex assured her.

"Something is burning, Tex," said Gran acerbically, and we watched the doctor hurry back to his grill and try to salvage what he could from the food being burned to a crisp.

"Good thing Marge always makes sure there's plenty of food to go around," said Brutus.

"Oh, Marge simply allows her husband to think he's the great grillmaster," I said. "But all the while she's the one who makes sure these barbecues are a success."

"So how about these collars?" asked Harriet, as she gestured to the gadget she still carried around her neck.

The company that made the collars had apologized profusely for the mishap. Turns out the data stream connected to the collars had entered the Mokemon universe, causing us to pop up on the players' displays as Mokemons. The mistake had been corrected, and we'd all faithfully worn our collars for the duration of the experiment, which was now almost over.

"This is the new world," said Brutus as he tugged at the collar, which was a little too tight. "Soon the whole of humanity will be outfitted with these trackers, and then all you need to do to know if you've got some kind of disease is to log into the app. Heart problems, cancer, kidney stones? It will show up right there on the screen, and your doctor will be able to call you in for further tests, based on that information."

"I don't know," I said. "It sounds a little far-fetched to me. And besides, how do you know these things won't get hacked, and those hackers will use your personal information for all kinds of nefarious purposes?"

"I'm sure it's all very safe and secure," said Brutus.

I distinctly remembered being chased up a tree by the Mokemon hunters, and so I wasn't a big believer in that so-called security. In fact I couldn't wait for the collar to come off again.

"I'm with Brutus," said Harriet, taking her boyfriend's side as usual. "If this thing works, we'll all live forever, and wouldn't that be great?"

"If I do live forever, I want us to be together always, you guys," said Dooley fervently.

This statement brought smiles to all of our faces, and as we watched on, we saw how Chase put his arm around Odelia's shoulder as they shared a warm smile. And how Tex placed the one sausage he'd been able to salvage on Marge's plate, who offered him a grateful smile, then scraped off the black crust when her husband wasn't looking.

Uncle Alec handed Charlene a piece of fish to sample, and she rewarded him with a tender hand placed on his cheek. And Scarlett and Gran, who were arguing again, suddenly burst into loud laughter, and it soon became clear to me that, like George and Anna, and even Tammy and Mark, or even Johnny and Jerry, love is everywhere, whether romantic love, or the love of friendship. And as Brutus tapped my shrinking belly and gave me a thumbs up for all of my hard work, I gave him a proud and thankful grin.

I might not have gotten my super high-tech pet flap, but that was love, too, with Odelia simply looking out for me. The way we all looked out for one another. Humans and cats. Okay, and maybe even dogs.

And isn't that what life is all about?

THE END

Thanks for reading! If you want to know when a new Nic Saint book comes out, sign up for Nic's mailing list: nicsaint.com/news

EXCERPT FROM BETWEEN A GHOST AND A SPOOKY PLACE (GHOSTS OF LONDON 1)

Chapter 1

"I didn't think you'd show up," the gruff voice announced.

Harry looked up from her perusal of the latest James Patterson. She quickly closed the book and shoved it into her backpack, then rose from her perch on the low wall of the underpass. She shrugged as she approached the hulking figure. "I'm always true to my word," she told the man, doing her best not to look or sound intimidated.

He really was a giant of a man, though she'd been told he wasn't as dangerous as he looked. He could have fooled her, though. He had no neck to speak of, his arms alone were probably as thick as her waist, and she could have fitted several times in the long black overcoat he was wearing, she herself being rather on the petite side.

She pushed her blond tresses from her brow and fixed her golden eyes on the stranger, rubbing her hands to keep warm. She'd removed her gloves and knitted cap and now thought perhaps she shouldn't have. The cold drizzle that had started overnight had turned into a real downpour, and even though they were protected from the brunt of the autumn weather by the underpass, the wet cold still crept in Harry's clothes and chilled her to the bone.

"Let's do this," the man grumbled. "I haven't got all day."

The watery sun that had tried to pierce the dark deck of clouds that afternoon had finally given up its struggle, giving free rein to the driving rain. But then this was London, a city that for some reason had collectively decided the sun had no business here, except on those very rare occasions.

She quickly unzipped the main compartment of her backpack and took out the package, then handed it to the client. Through the clear plastic protective cover it was easy to make out its contents, but the burly man insisted on taking the book out nonetheless.

"You're going to get it all smudged," Harry murmured, though she knew this was none of her business. Once the transaction was made, the book belonged to the client, to do with as they pleased, whether she liked it or not.

"Looking good," the man muttered, flipping through the pages of the voluminous tome. "How do I know it's the real deal?"

"You have Sir Buckley's word," she said with a light shrug.

The client scrutinized her carefully, shoving the book back into its plastic covering. Then he nodded once. "Good enough for me," he announced. He handed her a small black briefcase. "One million. As agreed," he told her.

She balanced the briefcase on her knee and clicked it open. Two thousand 500 pound notes should be there and as far as she could determine they were all present and accounted for. But then again, she didn't think the client was going to cheat her. And even if he did, Buckley would handle it.

So she clasped the briefcase under her arm and looked up at the man, a little trepidatious. Buckley had always told her to conclude the meeting the moment the transfer was done, and only rarely did a client linger. This one still stood staring at her, however, as if their business wasn't concluded yet. They were the only two people there, as the underpass was quite deserted.

This was Buckley's favorite place to make a transfer, as this particular spot wasn't covered by any of London's half a million cameras. Which also meant that if a client decided to get any funny ideas, Harry had no recourse. It wasn't as if she had a black belt in jujitsu or some other martial arts discipline. She'd recently watched a video on the Daily Mail website on how to protect yourself against an attack, but hadn't the foggiest notion how to execute those nifty self-defense moves in real life.

The man gave her an unexpected grin, displaying two gold teeth. It was something you didn't see that often these days, and she found herself staring at the shiny snappers before she could stop herself. Along with his bald dome, it gave him the aspect of an old-fashioned James Bond bad guy. But then his smile suddenly disappeared, and he gave her a curt nod. "I guess that concludes our business," he grunted.

"Yeah, I guess it does," she returned.

He abruptly flipped his hoodie over his head, then turned and walked away. Soon he was swallowed up by the shadows stretching long tendrils of darkness beneath the overpass. Moments later she heard a motorcycle kicking into gear, and then its roar as it raced away into the falling dusk.

She heaved a sigh of relief. These exchanges were going to be the death of her one day, she thought as she hurried out of the underpass, to where she'd fastened her bicycle to a streetlight. Fortunately, it was still where she'd left it. She tried to fit the entire suitcase into her backpack but failed, so she tipped its precious contents into her trusty Jack Wolfskin rucksack and dumped the suitcase in a nearby trashcan. And as she adjusted the straps, she noted a little giddily she'd never worn a million pounds on her back before. Then she pressed her pink knitted cap to her head, used her gloves to wipe that fabled London precipitation from her saddle, mounted the bike and was off.

Five minutes later she was pedaling down Newport Street, anxious to get back to the store. She'd only feel at ease once the money was safely transferred to Sir Geoffrey Buckley's cash register. And as she waited for the traffic light to turn green, she idly wondered what she would do with so much money. She could quit her job, buy herself a great house and take that trip around the world she'd been dreaming of for ages. The lights changed, and traffic was off and so was she, stomping down on her silly daydreams. The money wasn't hers and never would be. She was, after all, only a lowly wage slave in Sir Buckley's employ. Why there was a Sir in front of his name, she didn't know, even after working for the man for close to a year now.

Buckley Antiques, the store where she spent her days when her employer wasn't sending her to dark and creepy places to exchange packages with obscure and dangerous-looking clients, was a smallish shop tucked away in the more dingy part of Notting Hill. It carried rare antiques and other items for the connoisseur, its owner and proprietor, the eponymous Sir Geoffrey, priding himself in his capacity to obtain items for his clients that no other antiquarian could find. There was a whiff of the illegal and the criminal attached to both the man and the shop, and oftentimes Harry wondered where he obtained these rare and exclusive items if not by illicit means.

She'd never asked, and Buckley had never told her, of course. She merely did as she was told, and delivered million pound books to men with no necks without asking pesky questions. Such as: why would anyone buy a book for such an incredible price? And why not transfer the items at the store? She didn't ask because she was afraid she wouldn't particularly like the answer.

She couldn't help wonder, though, where the priceless tome would end up, for No-Neck, like Harry herself, was probably only the messenger.

But even though Harry knew that her employer was something of a high-end fence, her conscience was no match for her need of a regular paycheck.

With her history degree she didn't stand much of a chance to find a decent-paying job in London, or anywhere else in the United Kingdom for that matter, and she knew she should be grateful to have found a job at all that was a cut above being a waitress, cleaning lady or nanny. The job might not be completely on the up and up, but it was better than being on welfare.

Besides, for her discretion Buckley paid her a nice little stipend around the holidays, so there was that as well.

She attached her bike to the lantern in front of the store, and entered the shop, her trusty backpack burning with the money. As she stepped inside, the doorbell jangled merrily. As usual, the store was dimly lit, Buckley's way of adding atmosphere. She picked her way past the antique cupboards and Louis XIV armoires and tried to ignore the quite horrendous oil paintings adorning the walls. When she reached the counter, fully expecting to find Buckley pottering about, she was surprised to see him absent from the scene.

No sound could be heard, either, except for the ticking of a dozen antique Swiss cuckoo clocks Buckley had obtained from a Swiss traveling cuckoo clock salesman. A real bargain, he'd called them, though Harry failed to understand who'd ever want to pay good money for such monstrosities.

"Buckley?" she called out. "Buckley, I'm back!"

Usually the prospect of money brought out her employer like the genie from the bottle, but no frizzy-haired elderly gentleman popped up now.

Harry shrugged, and started transferring the money from her backpack to the cash register, which had a deep and convenient space beneath the money drawer. Here it would be quite safe until Buckley put it in the ancient but very sturdy vault he kept in his office.

She wondered briefly if she shouldn't close up the shop, as she wasn't even supposed to be working today. Buckley had called her in to deal with this urgent delivery, and she'd grudgingly complied. He didn't like to deal with his 'special clients' himself, reserving that particular privilege for her.

And it was as she stood wondering what to do when she became aware of a soft groaning sound coming from deeper into the shop. It seemed to come from the back. With a slight swing in her step, relieved to be rid of the huge pile of money, she decided to take a look. She didn't like to lock the door without Buckley's say-so. He had this thing about wanting the store to be open at all hours, even if that meant she had to take her lunch break in between serving customers. But she didn't like to leave it unattended either.

She would just have a look around and as soon as she'd found her employer—probably messing about somewhere in his office—she'd go home. After riding around in the rain for the past half hour she was wet, tired and numb, and a hot shower and some dry clothes looked pretty good right now.

Besides, she needed to put in some shopping and wanted to get it done before rush hour, hoping to salvage what little she could from her day off.

"Buckley?" she called out as she moved deeper into the store. Behind the showroom were two smaller rooms. One was Buckley's office, where he liked to meet with clients and suppliers, and the other was the small kitchen reserved for personnel—which meant her. It wasn't much. Just a table, some chairs, a sink, gas stove and fridge. Next to the kitchen a staircase led upstairs, to the apartment Buckley rented out for a stipend. In exchange, the man, who was rarely in during the day, kept an eye on the store after six.

"Buckley?" she tried again. She noticed that the door to his office was ajar, so she pushed it open. And that's when she saw her employer. He was stretched out on the floor, his limbs arranged in an awkward pose, blood pooling around his head. She clasped a hand to her face, her throat closed on a silent scream, and looked down at the lifeless body. It was obvious she was too late. His eyes were open and staring into space, his face pale as a sheet.

"Oh, Buckley, Buckley," she finally whispered hoarsely, automatically taking her phone from her pocket with quaking hand and dialing 999.

Minutes later, the store was abuzz with police and medics, as she sat nursing a cup of tea in the kitchen, stunned and fighting waves of nausea.

She looked up when she became aware of being watched, and she saw a man looking down at her from the entrance to the kitchen. He was tall and broad and easily filled the door-frame, both in width and height. She noted to her surprise that he was gazing at her with a scowl on his handsome face. Perfectly coiffed dark hair, steely gray eyes, chiseled features and an anvil jaw lent him classic good looks, and for a moment she thought none other than David Gandy himself had wandered into the store, mistaking it for the scene of his latest swimwear shoot. But then the man cleared his throat.

"Inspector Watley. Can I ask you a few questions, Miss McCabre?"

She nodded, wiping a tear from her eye. "Yes, of course, Inspector."

The inspector took a seat at the table and placed a small

notebook in front of him, checking it briefly. "Your name is Henrietta McCabre?"

"Yes, but most people just call me Harry," she said softly.

"You were the one who found the body, Miss McCabre?"

"Yes, I did," she said, tears once again brimming in her eyes.

"And what time was this?"

"Must have been... around four. I'd just come back from an errand."

He gave her a dark look. "An errand connected to the store?"

She nodded again. She was loathe to reveal the nature of her errand. Even dead, she didn't want to betray Buckley's confidence.

"Tell me exactly what you saw," Inspector Watley said gruffly.

She quickly told him what had happened, and didn't forget to mention the groan she'd heard—the sound which had alerted her of Buckley's presence.

Watley's frown deepened. "You heard a groan, you say?"

"Yes, I did. It's the reason I came back here. I thought Mr. Buckley had stepped out of the store, as he didn't respond when I called out. So when I heard the groan, I went looking for him... And that's when I found him."

"That's odd," the inspector said, fixing her with an intent stare.

"What is?"

"The groan."

"Why odd? It is perfectly natural for someone who's just tumbled and knocked his head to groan. I'm just surprised I didn't hear it sooner."

"According to the preliminary findings of our coroner, Mr. Buckley must have been dead for at least half an hour before you arrived, Miss McCabre."

This news startled her. "He was dead... before I arrived?"

"Yes, he was."

"Oh, poor Mr. Buckley," she said. "To think he'd been lying there all this time before I found him! If only I'd arrived sooner, he could've been saved." She looked at the policeman. "I knew this would happen. I just knew it."

He stared at her blankly. "You knew he was going to die?"

She nodded. "He was very unsteady on his feet lately. Only last month he took quite a tumble when he stepped from the store. I told him he should get a cane, but he was far too proud." She shook her head, extremely distraught. "It was only a matter of time before he took a bad fall and hit his head."

The policeman eyed her curiously for a moment, then lowered his head and said slowly, "Your employer didn't hit his head, Miss McCabre."

"What do you mean? If he didn't hit his head, then how did he die?"

"Mr. Buckley was murdered, Miss McCabre. Murdered in cold blood with a blunt object by the looks of things." Then, without waiting a beat, he went on, "Can you account for your whereabouts between the hours of three and four, Miss McCabre?"

Her jaw dropped. Was he accusing her of murdering her own boss? "Well, I wasn't here if that's what you mean," she was quick to point out.

"Where were you then?"

And she was about to respond when she remembered she couldn't. Even though providing herself with an alibi was more important than respecting Mr. Buckley's wishes, she still couldn't tell the inspector where she'd been. Not if she didn't want to get in big trouble with No-Neck and his employer.

Chapter 2

It didn't take a genius to figure out she was in a pickle. Not only didn't she have an alibi, but apparently the safe was empty, all of Mr. Buckley's possessions stolen. It was obvious how things looked from Scotland Yard's point of view. They probably figured she'd burgled the safe, seeing as she knew the combination, was caught in the act by her employer, at which point a violent struggle had ensued and she'd violently slain the older man. The only reason she wasn't being placed under arrest was that she'd be an idiot to stick around after the murder, or to call the police herself.

These and other thoughts were now swirling in Harry's head as Inspector Watley told her tersely to please remain available for questioning—probably the Scotland Yard equivalent for 'Don't leave town!'

She nodded quickly, her face now completely devoid of color and her extremities of blood, and wobbly got to her feet the minute Watley left.

And as she made her way out of the store, which was still swarming with police, she feebly wondered what she was going to do now. For one thing, she was most definitely out of a job. Which was something she should have told Watley, she now saw. Clearly she had no motive for murder; it simply meant unemployment. Then again, she'd just tucked a million pounds of motive into the shop till, and who knew how much more money Buckley kept in his safe, along with countless other valuables? Plenty of motive there.

As she rode her bicycle home, the rain was coming down again in sheets, and even before she'd reached the street where she lived, she was soaked to the skin. A fitting ending to a lousy day, she thought miserably.

Arriving home at Valentine Street No. 9, she quickly fastened her bike to the cellar window grille, wiped the rain from her eyes, and jogged up the steps to the front door. Letting herself in, she stood leaking rainwater on the black and white checkered floor for a moment, then slammed the heavy door shut, and quickly checked the mailbox. A magazine had arrived—the historical magazine she subscribed to —and a bill from the electric company, probably announcing another rate hike.

She hurried up the stairs, already shucking off her jacket, and when she arrived on the landing wasn't surprised to find her neighbor patiently awaiting her arrival, Harry's snowy white Persian in her arms.

"Oh, shoot," she said, taking the cat from the elderly lady. "Did Snuggles sneak into your flat again, Mrs. Peak? I thought I locked her up this time."

Mrs. Peak, the wizened old prune-faced lady who lived next door, gave her a wistful smile. "I don't mind, Harry. I only wish she visited me more often. I wouldn't mind having a darling like Snuggles myself, you know."

"Perhaps one day you will," said Harry as she pulled Snuggles's ear. "If she keeps this up, I just might have to give her away."

Mrs. Peak didn't seem to mind one bit. "Snuggles can drop by any time," she assured her.

"Thank you, Mrs. Peak," she said, letting herself into her flat. And as she closed the door, she whispered, "What's the matter with you, little one? Why do you keep sneaking off to the neighbors, huh? Don't you like it here?"

She put the cat down on the floor and looked around her modest flat. It wasn't even a flat, really, more of a studio apartment. One living room with kitchenette, a small bedroom, and an even smaller bathroom. Just enough for the student she'd been when she took it, and currently all she could afford on her meager earnings. She'd told herself back then that once she got her first paycheck she was going to find something bigger. But then she'd seen the paltry sum on her paycheck and had realized that it would be a long time before she'd be able to afford anything more than what she had. In fact she was lucky to have a place as nice as this one, London quickly becoming too costly for anyone without a millionaire mum or dad to foot the bill.

She watched as Snuggles haughtily stalked to the window, which was open to a crack, hopped out onto the small balcony, and started to make her way over to Mrs. Peak again. Harry quickly hurried after her and managed to snatch her just before she hopped from her balcony to the next.

"What's wrong with you?" she asked as she took the cat indoors again and closed the window. "Do you get special treats next door? Is that it?"

She checked Snuggles's bowl, but it was still filled to capacity. Possibly she was simply bored with the same dry food and needed something fresh?

And she was just scooping some canned food into a second bowl, much to Snuggles's delight, when she remembered she'd scheduled a call with her cousin.

She hurried over to her laptop, flipped it open and switched it on. And as she made herself a jam sandwich and carried it on a plate to the laptop, she kicked off her soggy sneakers, then hopped into the bedroom to change into something dry. She was just wrapping a towel around her head when the telltale sound of Skype warned her that Alice was online and calling her.

Video image of her cousin flickered to life, and she gave her a jolly wave.

"Hey, honey," Alice said. "Did you just step out of the shower?"

"No, I just stepped out of London, which is basically the same thing."

Alice laughed. She was a perky blonde with remarkable green eyes, and perennially in a good mood. "You should come and visit, Harry. It's about eighty degrees out here and not a single cloud in sight."

Harry sighed. "That sounds like heaven. I wish I could, but..."

"The antique shop, huh? Too much work? I can relate, honey. I'm actually holding down three jobs right now if you can believe it. The mortuary, the gun store, *and* the bakery. Never worked so hard in my life!" Harry nodded absently, and Alice's face fell. "Are you all right? You look very pale."

She shook her head. "Something horrible happened to me today, Alice."

She proceeded to tell her cousin about the murder of her boss, and Alice cried, "Oh, no! You must have been terrified! How are you holding up?"

"I'm... fine, actually. Though at the moment I seem to be the only suspect the police have." She tucked a leg beneath her and told Alice the whole story.

She and her cousin had no secrets from each other. They'd always been close, ever since Alice's father, Curtis Whitehouse, had been stationed in London, working at Scotland Yard in an advisory capacity for five years. Since Uncle Curtis and Aunt Demitria had lived right next door to Harry's parents, she and Alice had been like sisters. The bond had never been broken, even now, when they were thousands of miles apart.

"So they think you have something to do with the murder?"

"Judging from the look on Inspector Watley's face, yes. And I can't even give him an alibi, as my client would never forgive me."

"Who is he?"

She shrugged. "Probably some rich businessman who

doesn't want to pay full price for his works of art. Most of them are, Buckley once told me."

"Can't you ask? This No-Neck person must be traceable, right?"

"Actually I have no idea how to get in touch with him. Buckley always made all the arrangements. I just had to show up to make the exchange."

"If I were you I'd try to find the guy," Alice suggested. "Otherwise you're in big trouble, honey. The police will be very suspicious if you won't tell them where you were." She shook her head. "Oh, how I wish I could help you."

She didn't see how she could, though. Even though Alice's father was now chief of police in the small town where he and his family lived, he had no clout with Scotland Yard. Unless...

"Does your father still keep in touch with his old colleagues?"

"He might," Alice admitted. "Do you want me to ask him?"

"Could you? Perhaps if I can just talk to someone, I can explain what happened without betraying the client's confidence."

"All right. Sit tight, hon. I'll give him a call now." Then she paused, looking thoughtful. "You know? There's actually someone else who might be able to help you."

Harry took a bite from her sandwich. She suddenly found she was starving. "There is? Who?"

"He's, um..." Alice bit her lip. "He's a guy who knows people, you know."

"Yes?"

Alice stared at her for a beat. "I'll have to discuss it with him first, though."

"Okay," she said, a little puzzled. It wasn't like Alice to suddenly go all mysterious on her. "Is he from England?"

"No, he's American, but he might know someone over

there who can help you." She eyed her anxiously. "I worry about you. You're all alone out there."

"I'll be fine," she said, though she realized that she didn't sound very convincing. It was true that she was quite alone out here. Her parents had died in a car crash the day of her graduation, and since she didn't have any sisters or brothers she basically had to rely on herself. She had an aunt and uncle up in Scotland but hadn't heard from them in ages. The only family she kept in touch with was Alice, which was at least something to be thankful for.

Alice seemed to make up her mind. "I'm going to talk to Brian. I'm going to ask him to pull a few strings."

"Oh, okay," she said. "Who's Brian?"

Alice closed her lips, her face turning red. "I, um, didn't I mention him?"

"No, you didn't." She laughed. "What? Is he, like, your new boyfriend or something?"

"No, of course not! Reece and I are still very much together. You know that."

Alice was engaged to Reece Hudson, a famous movie star. Even Harry had seen a couple of his movies. He was a great guy and loved to goof around with Harry when he and Alice came to London. The couple usually stayed at the Ritz-Carlton, just about the swankiest place Harry had ever seen. Reece wasn't impressed, though. Said he'd stayed in far more luxurious hotels in other parts of the world. Which just went to show how the other half lived.

"Look, I've gotta go," Alice suddenly said.

All this talk about this mysterious Brian had apparently made her nervous, for she flinched when Harry protested, "You still haven't told me who this Brian guy is."

"I'll tell you all about him, honey. But first I need to get him to agree to something." She gave her a long look before asking her the most outrageous question of all. "Do you still… see things, Harry?"

She frowned. "See things? What do you mean? What things?"

"You know. When we were kids, sometimes you used to tell me you saw people who weren't really there, remember? Like… dead people?"

She laughed. "Come on, Alice. You know that was just my overactive imagination."

"No, but you said you saw Gran, remember? You even talked to her."

She did remember, though only vaguely. It was true that when her and Alice's grandmother had passed away, she'd imagined seeing her, after she had supposedly passed on. The old lady had visited ten-year-old Harry's bedroom the night she died. She'd told her that everything would be fine, and that she was moving on to a different plane but that she'd always watch over her and Alice. Later she'd begun to think she'd imagined the whole thing.

"You know that was just a dream," she told her cousin, but Alice didn't seem convinced. "I mean, what else could it have been, right?"

A slight smile played about her cousin's lips, but then she nodded. "Yeah, probably a dream. Anyway, I've got to go."

"Let me know what your father has to say, all right? I really hope he knows someone on this side I can talk to."

"Will do, honey. Love you! Bye-bye!"

She rang off and stared out the window for a while. The rain was lashing the single pane, and the sky was pitch black, even though it wasn't even fully evening yet. Snuggles jumped on her lap and installed herself there, purring contentedly. She stroked her behind the ears. "So it was the food, huh?" she murmured as she settled back.

She thought about what Alice had said about Brian, and

wondered what that was all about. But then she figured it had nothing to do with her, and decided not to expect too much. Alice had a habit of making a lot of promises before promptly forgetting all about them. And seeing as she was so busy, it would be a small miracle if she even remembered to ask her father about his Scotland Yard contacts. If he still had any left. It'd been almost ten years since he'd returned to the States and became Happy Bays's chief of police.

She thought back to Inspector Watley, and the dark looks he'd given her. It was obvious that if it were up to him, he'd have arrested her on the spot.

She heaved a deep sigh. "We're in deep trouble, Snuggles," she murmured. "If things don't look up it's not such a bad idea to head on over to Mrs. Peak for your kibble. She might just be your new owner from now on."

She shivered and moved over to the window to close the curtains. For the first time in a long time she didn't have anywhere to be the next day.

Chapter 3

Jarrett Zephyr-Thornton III was perfecting his ice skating technique when his personal valet beckoned him from the side of the rink. As per his instructions, the rink had been closed off to the public to allow Jarrett to practice in private. It was his dream to become the next big thing in figure skating, and since he'd never been on the skates before, but he'd seen all the movies, he knew that practice made perfect, so practice it was.

He was a spindly young man with wavy butter-colored hair and pale blue eyes that regarded the world with child-like wonder. As the son of the richest man in England he was in the unique position to do whatever he wanted whenever he wanted to do it, and what he wanted more than anything right now was to be the next British figure skating Olympic champion.

He groaned in annoyance when he caught sight of his valet Deshawn's urgent wave. "I told you to hold all my calls!" he cried, but the music pounding from the speakers drowned out his voice. It was the soundtrack of *Ice Princess*, of course, playing on a loop. Motivation was key, he knew, and he watched the movie at least once a day to keep him in the right frame of mind.

Reluctantly he finished his pirouette and swished over to the side.

"Yes, yes, yes," he grumbled when Deshawn handed him the phone. "This is Jarrett!" he called out pleasantly when it was finally pressed to his ear. "Oh, it's you, Father," he said with an exaggerated eye roll. "What am I doing?" He frowned at Deshawn, who shrugged. Father never asked him what he was doing. Just as Jarrett made it his aim in life to do as little as possible, his pater made it his habit to interfere as infrequently as possible, lest he develop a heart condition. "I'm ice skating, if you must know," he said a little huffily, fully expecting a barrage of criticism to be poured into his ear at this confession. "For what? The Olympic Games, of course. What else?"

"Look, son, something's come up," the author of his being now grated in his ear. "I need you to listen to me and listen to me very carefully, you hear?"

He did listen very carefully, even though he was quite sure that whatever the old man had to impart was probably a load of poppycock as usual. "Yes, Father. I am listening," he announced with another eye roll. There was a crackling noise on the other end, and then his father said, "I need you or that valet of yours to go over to…" There was that crackle again.

"There seems to be some sort of noise. What did you just say?"

"I need you to pick up the parcel and bring it to..."

"I'm losing you," he said, quickly losing patience.

"The parcel is at... right now, and if you don't pick it up... it's going to... along with your mother's... and that'll be the end of..."

"You're not making any sense," he said, staring down at his nice new blue spandex outfit. He'd bought seven, a different color for each day of the week. He particularly liked the one he was wearing now. It looked exactly like the one Michelle Trachtenberg, the star of *Ice Princess*, wore in the movie. "What package? And what does Mother have to do with anything?"

"Will you just listen!" the old man yelled, now audibly irritated. "If you don't pick up that package right now... then... and... unmitigated disaster!"

He sighed. Whatever his old man was involved in, it could probably wait, so he said, "First get decent reception, Father, and call me back, all right?"

And he deftly clicked off the phone and handed it back to Deshawn. He then gave his valet a look of warning. "No more phone calls, Deshawn."

Deshawn, a rather thickset smallish man with perfectly coiffed thinning brown hair and an obsequious manner, had been in Jarrett's employ for many years, and the two formed rather an odd couple. One thin and tall, the other short and stout, they resembled Laurel & Hardy in their heyday.

The valet now muttered, "I know, sir. My apologies. But your father said it was extremely urgent."

"It's always urgent," said Jarrett with an airy wave of the hand. "But he'll just have to wait, for I..." He glided away. "... am on my way to greatness!"

And with these words, he allowed the wonderful music of

Ice Princess to guide him back onto the rink and launch him into his most complicated movement yet: the twizzle, a one-foot turn. He usually worked with Vance Crowdell, trainer to the stars, but the man had some other arrangement tonight, so he'd been forced to train alone. Not that he minded. The crusty old trainer had already taught him so many new movements he needed to practice until he'd perfected those before learning any new ones.

And as he closed his eyes and allowed the music to take him into a new and wonderful world of glitter and glamor and thunderous applause, he saw himself as the first male Olympic figure skating gold medalist to come out of Britain in quite a long time.

Philo eyed the woman darkly. "I'm not asking, Madame Wu. I'm telling you. Take the package and hand it over as soon as you're told."

"But I can't," the proprietress of Xing Ming lamented in nasal tones. Her jet-black hair clearly came from a bottle and her horn-rimmed glasses were too large for her narrow face. She'd been running the small family restaurant for thirty years, one of the mainstays of London's Chinatown in the City of Westminster. "I have other matters tonight. I can't do package right now."

He thrust the package back into her hands. "Just take it already. Lives depend on this," he added with a meaningful look. A look that said it was her own life that depended on it.

She rattled the package, her eyes unnaturally large behind the glasses. "What is it? Is it bomb?"

"No, is not bomb," he said, mimicking her accent. "It's just something very important." He leaned in. "Very important to Master Edwards."

A look of fear stole over her face, and she nodded quickly. "Yes, yes. Master Edwards. I will hand over package no problem. Hand over who?"

"You'll know her when you see her."

"Is woman?"

"Apparently."

Actually he didn't know himself. All he knew was that his contact had told him he would send his assistant, and she would be dressed in black. But since no one else knew about the package he wasn't too worried. He pointed a stubby finger at Madame Wu. "Just make sure she gets it, all right?"

She nodded, tucking the package beneath the counter. "Of course, Philo."

And as he stepped from the restaurant, the smell of Chinese food in his nostrils, he shook his head. Used to be that people like Madame Wu wouldn't dare contradict him, but that was before Master Edwards had fallen ill. The rumor that the old man was on the verge of death was spreading fast, and already his criminal empire was crumbling and his influence waning.

He crossed the busy street, bright neon lights announcing all manner of Asian food from every corner, and mounted the motorcycle he used to get around London in a hurry. And then he was off, narrowly missing the entry into the Chinese restaurant of a slender woman, all dressed in black.

It didn't take him long to race across town to his employer's house, in the heart of the East End. Master Edwards's house was located in a gated community, his own people providing protection, and Philo nodded to the guard as he passed. He'd hired him personally. A short drive up the hill led him to the house at the end of the street, which towered over all others. It used to belong to a famous actor in the sixties and was a sprawling mansion with fifty rooms, an underground pool, and cinema where Edwards and his cronies enjoyed watching gangster movies. Or rather, that's how it used to be.

He parked his bike in the garage and mounted the stairs, deftly making his way upstairs until he reached the landing and heard the telltale sounds of Master Edwards's snoring. Entering the bedroom, where the bedridden gang leader was laid up, he wasn't surprised to find him sound asleep. The moment he flicked on the light, the old man awoke with a start.

"Philo!" he muttered, blinking against the light. "Is that you?"

"It is, Master."

A look of annoyance crept into the man's eyes. "Why did you wake me?"

"Just to tell you that the package is being delivered as we speak."

The man's irritability dwindled. "Good," he said, settling back against the pillow. "Very good. Let's just hope the book works as advertised."

"I'm sure it will."

The old man licked his dry lips. "A lot depends on this, Philo. But then I probably don't need to remind you."

No, he didn't. He'd reminded him plenty of times since the chain of events had been set in motion a fortnight ago.

"There's only one small matter left to attend to," he said.

Master Edwards, whose eyes had drooped shut, opened them again. "Mh? What's that?"

"There's a witness," he said. "A young woman by the name of Henrietta McCabre. She's seen my face and might possibly become a nuisance."

"So?" snapped Master Edwards. "Just get it done, Philo. You don't need my permission to handle such a minor detail."

"No, Master," he said deferentially, though of course he did need the other's permission. In Master Edwards's world nothing ever happened without his approval, and most definitely not something of this importance.

"See to it that she's silenced, Philo. And make sure nobody sees you this time," the old man snapped, before closing his eyes once again. Soft snores soon sounded from the bed, and Philo bowed his head and retreated from the bedroom of his employer of twenty-five years. In this, the man's final days, he wasn't about to disappoint him. Not if he valued his own life. Henrietta McCabre, whoever she was, would not see her next birthday, he would make sure of that. And as he stalked over to his own room in the mansion, he sat down at the computer to begin an intense study of the life of Henrietta 'Harry' McCabre. This time, there would be no mistakes. And no witnesses.

,

ABOUT NIC

Nic has a background in political science and before being struck by the writing bug worked odd jobs around the world (including but not limited to massage therapist in Mexico, gardener in Italy, restaurant manager in India, and Berlitz teacher in Belgium).

When he's not writing he enjoys curling up with a good (comic) book, watching British crime dramas, French comedies or Nancy Meyers movies, sampling pastry (apple cake!), pasta and chocolate (preferably the dark variety), twisting himself into a pretzel doing morning yoga, going for a run, and spoiling his big red tomcat Tommy.

He lives with his wife (and aforementioned cat) in a small village smack dab in the middle of absolutely nowhere and is probably writing his next 'Mysteries of Max' book right now.

www.nicsaint.com

Purrfect Patsy

Purrfect Son

Purrfect Fool

Purrfect Fitness

Purrfect Setup

Purrfect Sidekick

Purrfect Deceit

Purrfect Ruse

Purrfect Swing

Purrfect Cruise

Purrfect Harmony

Purrfect Sparkle

Purrfect Cure

Purrfect Cheat

Purrfect Catch

The Mysteries of Max Box Sets

The Mysteries of Max Shorts

Purrfect Santa (3 shorts in one)

Purrfectly Flealess

Purrfect Wedding

Nora Steel

Murder Retreat

The Kellys

Murder Motel

Death in Suburbia

Emily Stone

Murder at the Art Class

Washington & Jefferson

First Shot

Alice Whitehouse

Spooky Times

Spooky Trills

Spooky End

Spooky Spells

Ghosts of London

Between a Ghost and a Spooky Place

Public Ghost Number One

Ghost Save the Queen

Box Set 1 (Books 1-3)

A Tale of Two Harrys

Ghost of Girlband Past

Ghostlier Things

Charleneland

Deadly Ride

Final Ride

Neighborhood Witch Committee

Witchy Start

Witchy Worries

Witchy Wishes

Saffron Diffley

Crime and Retribution

Vice and Verdict

Felonies and Penalties (Saffron Diffley Short 1)

The B-Team

Once Upon a Spy

Tate-à-Tate

Enemy of the Tates

Ghosts vs. Spies

The Ghost Who Came in from the Cold

Witchy Fingers

Witchy Trouble

Witchy Hexations

Witchy Possessions

Witchy Riches

Box Set 1 (Books 1-4)

The Mysteries of Bell & Whitehouse

One Spoonful of Trouble

Two Scoops of Murder

Three Shots of Disaster

Box Set 1 (Books 1-3)

A Twist of Wraith

A Touch of Ghost

A Clash of Spooks

Box Set 2 (Books 4-6)

The Stuffing of Nightmares

A Breath of Dead Air

An Act of Hodd

Box Set 3 (Books 7-9)

A Game of Dons

Standalone Novels

When in Bruges

The Whiskered Spy

ThrillFix

Homejacking

The Eighth Billionaire

The Wrong Woman

Made in the USA
Middletown, DE
05 July 2021